Bad Bot

Bad Bot

Pierrette Dubé

Illustrations by Vigg

Translated from the French by
David Warriner

SHiVeRs

ORCA BOOK PUBLISHERS

Published in English in Canada and the United States in 2024 by Orca Book Publishers.
orcabook.com

Library and Archives Canada Cataloguing in Publication
Title: Bad bot / Pierrette Dubé ; illustrations by Vigg ;
translated from the French by David Warriner
Other titles: Bête a pile. English
Names: Dubé, Pierrette, 1952– author. |
Warriner, David (Linguist), translator. | Vigg, 1972- illustrator.
Description: Series statement: Orca Shivers ; 2 | Translation of: La bête a pile.
Identifiers: Canadiana (print) 20230577016 | Canadiana (ebook) 20230577024 |
ISBN 9781459839830 (softcover) | ISBN 9781459839847 (PDF) | ISBN 9781459839854 (EPUB)
Subjects: LCGFT: Horror fiction. | LCGFT: Novels.
Classification: LCC PS8557.U2325 B4813 2024 | DDC jC843/.54—dc23

Library of Congress Control Number: 2023949571

Summary: In this short horror novel for middle-grade readers, lonely Victor befriends his new toy robot, LenBot. But when LenBot starts learning more than Victor has taught it, Victor realizes his new friend might be dangerous.

Orca Book Publishers is committed to reducing the consumption of nonrenewable resources in the making of our books. We make every effort to use materials that support a sustainable future.

Orca Book Publishers gratefully acknowledges the support for its publishing programs provided by the following agencies: the Government of Canada, the Canada Council for the Arts and the Province of British Columbia through the BC Arts Council and the Book Publishing Tax Credit.

We acknowledge the financial support of the Government of Canada through the National Translation Program for Book Publishing, an initiative of the *Roadmap for Canada's Official Languages 2013–2018: Education, Immigration, Communities*, for our translation activities.

Cover design by Troy Cunningham.
Edited by Gabrielle Prendergast.
Illustrations by Vigg.
Translated by David Warriner.

Printed and bound in Canada.

27 26 25 24 • 1 2 3 4

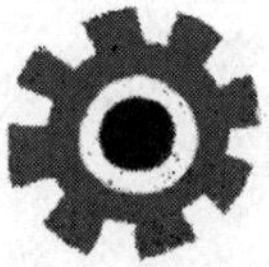

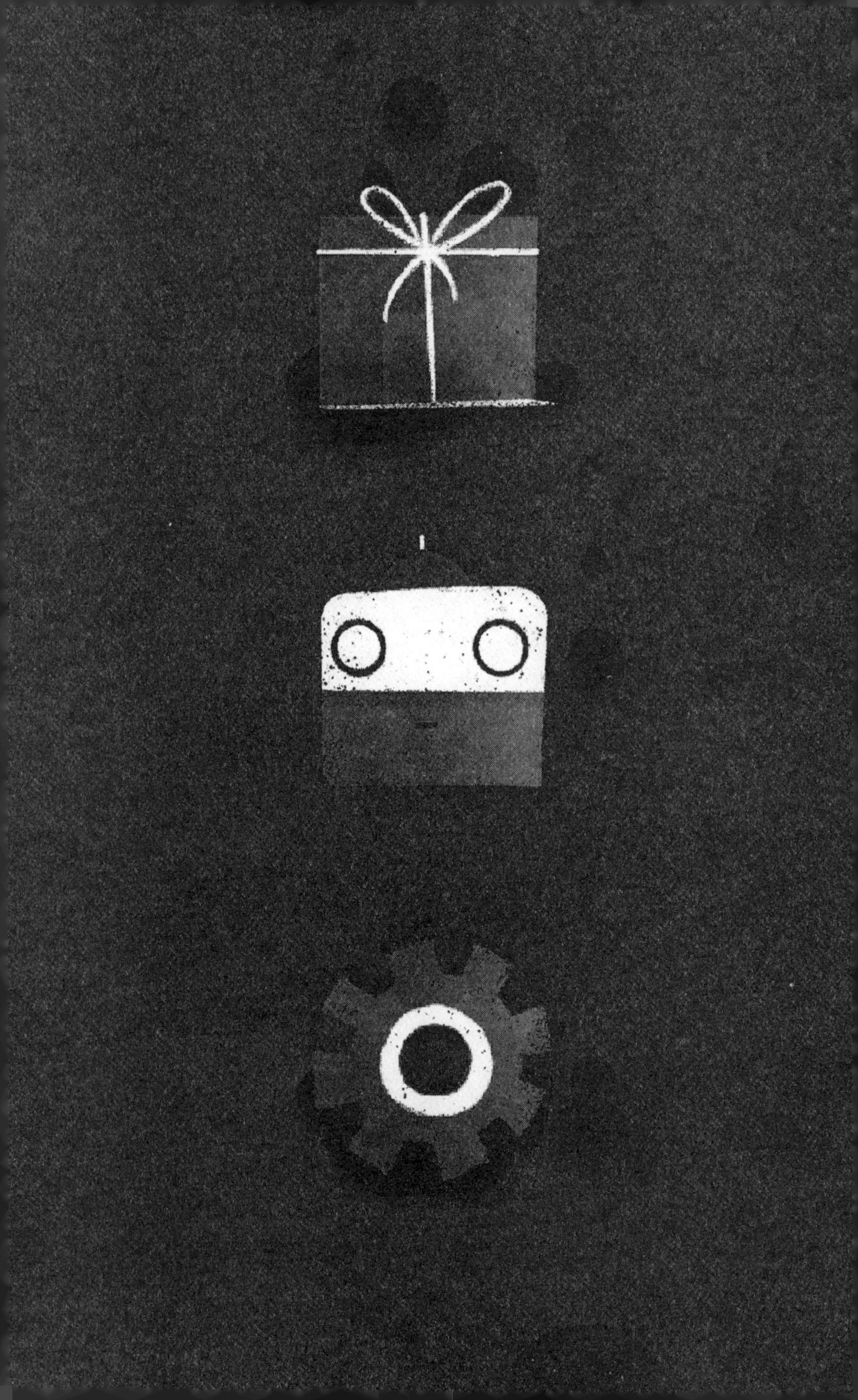

1

When I opened my big present on Christmas Day, I was over the moon!

"Yay! It's the smart robot I've been asking for!"

I'd first seen a LenBot (that's the name of this cute little contraption) at a friend's house—and I was smitten. I just had to have one of my own!

Obviously I would have preferred a dog.

"They're too much work," my mom said.

"Too dirty," said my dad.

It was true. In our minimalist apartment—all leather, chrome and brushed steel—there was no place for even the tiniest dog hair.

I persuaded my parents that a mini robot would be the perfect compromise. It had all the benefits of a pet and none of the hassles.

And so, in October, I very subtly started my Smart Robot for Christmas campaign. I played up all of LenBot's qualities. LenBot was smart, funny, endearing—and more. I stepped up my efforts in November. "A smart robot is a great way for kids to learn about coding," I told my parents. I have to admit, by the time December came around, my reasoning was verging on harassment.

I really earned my present this Christmas. It took three months of hard work to make it happen.

I couldn't wait to take my LenBot out of the box and show everyone.

This programmable mini robot was a strange little thing. Its screen could display a wide range of facial expressions. Its arms had joints and pincers at the ends. And it had enormous wheels on its sides. It wasn't very tall (not much bigger than a cup of coffee), but it looked and felt very solid.

"He does look very friendly," my mom said.

My grandpa Jean-Paul (I like to call him JP) cringed. Obviously he wasn't convinced. He just muttered through his triple-tone beard (black, gray and white), "You'd be better off playing outside."

I started reading the user manual right away.

Congratulations! You've made the smart choice with LenBot, the friendliest robot of them all! LenBot has 4 motors, 55 gears, 310 components and 45 facial expressions! Want to switch him on? Nothing could be simpler!

JP came over to me. "Show me that thing," he said. "I'll help you get started."

JP used to be an engineer. He's not afraid of technology. It wasn't a very complicated process. I downloaded the app to the old tablet my dad had given me. Then, with a few taps of the screen, my robot whirred to life.

"Lunch is ready!" my dad called a second later.

"Noooo, not now!" I protested.

"You can't play with him until he's finished charging anyway," JP said.

The meal seemed like it would never end. Out of the corner of my eye, I could see that my robot's indicator lights had turned green. That meant LenBot was fully charged and ready to go. Now he was just waiting for me!

I went right to my room as soon as my parents let me leave the table. I couldn't wait to see what my robot could do.

On the first page of the user manual, it said, in giant letters:

> **Meet Lenbot,**
> **Your New Best Friend**

Really? My new best friend? I was naive enough to believe it.

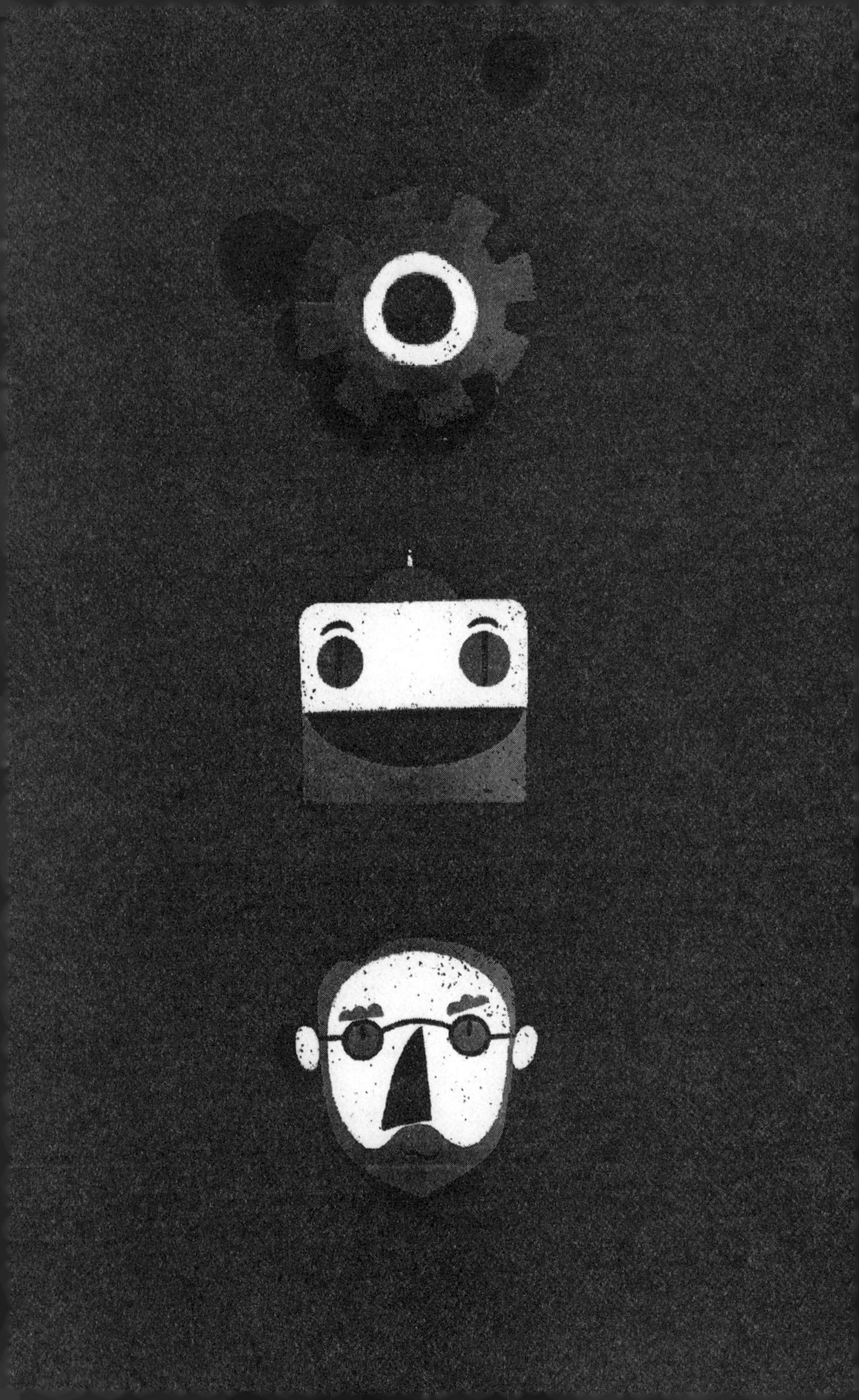

2

I had a best friend already, and his name was Ali. But his mom had been transferred abroad for a new job a few months back, so Ali and his family had moved away. Ali wouldn't be coming back here before the summer. In the meantime, we only got to see each other on video calls. I really missed Ali. Maybe that's why my robot ended up being such a big part of my life so quickly.

I'd been playing with LenBot for a few minutes when JP came into my room. I was so proud of what I could do with my new toy already. "Look at this, JP, it's amazing!"

I put LenBot down on the floor, and he paced all around the room before coming back to me.

"That gadget of yours is pretty neat," JP admitted.

"And that's not all. Look!" I bent down in front of the screen so LenBot could scan my face. Then I tapped my name into the app on my tablet.

VICTOR

LenBot seemed to get quite excited. Then he said triumphantly, "HI, VICTOR!"

"Ta-da! And that's just one of the things he can do. I can teach him all kinds of things. He can remember everything!"

It seems ridiculous now, looking back, but in that moment I was so excited. As if something important had just happened. Something that was going to change my life. Well, I wasn't wrong about that.

Next I tapped in my grandpa's name.

"HELLO, JEAN-PAUL," my robot said politely.

LenBot seemed to understand that I was his "friend" and JP was just a guest.

JP went downstairs to join my parents in the living room, and I kept on exploring LenBot's different functions. Not even an hour later, LenBot could already do lots of the basic things described in the user manual. He could carry blocks and stack them up, move in a straight line, obey orders, play some little games and even play music.

I heard my parents calling my name. It was time for dessert.

"So how's your new robot?" my dad asked me.

"Amazing! LenBot's fantastic!"

"That's what I'm worried about!" JP groaned.

I didn't really understand what he meant by that, not then. As usual, JP could see where things were going long before I did.

"How about we play some chess, kiddo?" he suggested after dessert.

It was the kind of offer I wouldn't normally refuse. I hesitated. "Maybe later," I replied.

I didn't want to say anything, but I had seen in the user manual that you could play chess with LenBot. I was looking forward to trying that function.

JP seemed disappointed. He left me alone with my robot and went back to the living room.

I spent the rest of the day playing with LenBot. When JP went home, my dad had to drag me out of my room to come and say goodbye.

I did as I was told, as quickly as I could. LenBot was right on my heels, going **BEEP, BEEP!** impatiently.

JP could tell I was keen to get away. For a split second, I felt sad for him. But I soon put that thought out of my mind.

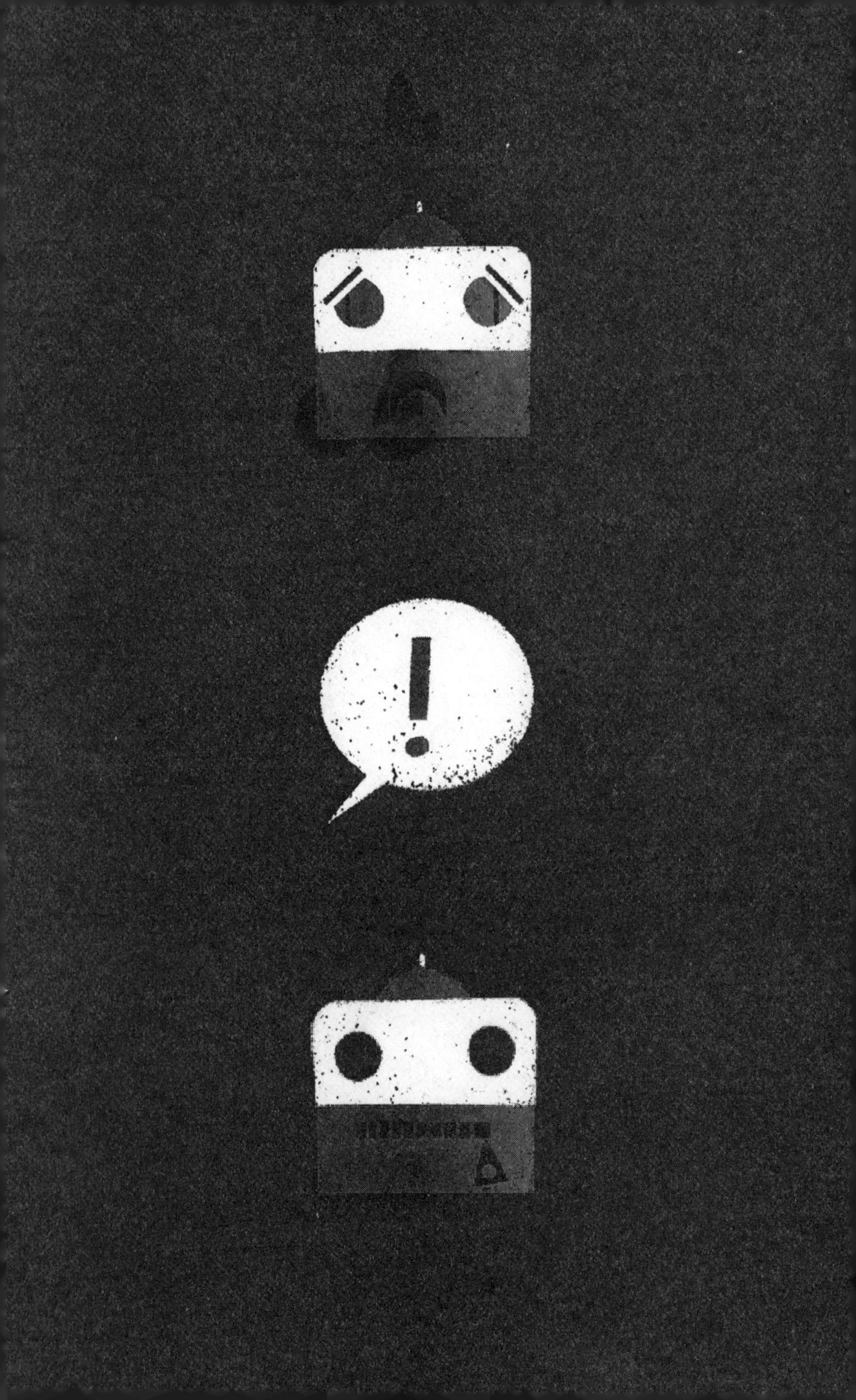

3

I spent my entire Christmas holidays with LenBot by my side. Whenever we went out to do something fun as a family—to watch a movie or go skating or cross-country skiing—all I could think about was getting home and seeing my robot again.

LenBot's knowledge was quite basic. He knew how to say a few simple phrases. He could do some different moves and play some easy games. I could have been happy with that, but I had big ambitions for my little bot.

It wasn't long before I turned to the Programming for Beginners section of the user manual. Here's how it started. **Follow these simple steps, and you can take your smart robot to a whole new level.**

LenBot was the perfect student. I taught him all kinds of fancy moves and tricks. I taught him some new words and even some songs. He made a lot of progress very quickly. I was proud of myself and my programming skills. Everything my robot could do was because I'd taught him.

Soon I decided to tackle the advanced section of the user manual.

At first my parents were happy I liked my present so much, but now they thought I was getting a little obsessed.

"Why don't you do something different for once, Victor? You barely go outside anymore. You don't get any exercise either. You don't draw. You don't read."

One day my aunt and uncle invited me to go snowboarding with my cousins Juliette and Alexia. My parents agreed right away, without asking me. They were probably desperate for me to get some fresh air.

"And you're not bringing that robot of yours!" my mom told me.

I figured I had no choice. And it wasn't that big a deal, really. I liked hanging out with my cousins.

But a day without LenBot?

My bot looked so sad when I told him the news.

"LENBOT TOO," he mumbled.

I knew he was just a toy and that his sad face was one of his 45 preprogrammed facial expressions (number 5, according to the user manual), but still, I felt a twinge of guilt.

"Sorry, you can't come with me. My parents said no."

This was the first time that my robot was not happy to obey my command. It was also the first time he'd expressed a wish of his own. I thought it was cute.

But I stood my ground. My bot tried to tug at my heartstrings.

"LENBOT FRIEND!" he chirped.

Aw, he was so adorable. But LenBot was just a toy. It was up to me to decide.

After a minute of silence, I thought my robot had given up. But then the sad face flashed off his screen and a cunning smile flashed up instead (facial expression 32). LenBot had an idea.

"HIDE!"

It was too tempting. I couldn't resist. I didn't really like disobeying my parents, but at the same time, it wouldn't hurt anyone if I brought him with me.

"All right, then. But only if you don't move and you don't say a word."

The cunning smile gave way to zipped lips (facial expression 23). I understood. This was our secret.

I slipped LenBot into the inside pocket of my parka. He kept his promise and didn't move or make a sound all afternoon. But I couldn't resist talking about him the whole time. "LenBot can do this, LenBot can do that…" Every time I said his name, I could feel LenBot vibrating contentedly in my pocket.

"If he's really that great, you should have brought him with you. You could have at least shown us," Juliette snapped.

There was no way I could tell her that LenBot was actually right there, hidden in my pocket.

That night I had a video call with my friend Ali. He was really into tech stuff. I told him about the awesome things my robot could do.

"I swear, he said 'LenBot too!' That means he can string together the words I've taught him to come up with his own ideas. Isn't that amazing?"

"That's super impressive," Ali agreed. "I didn't know LenBots had machine-learning capability. That means the machine can learn by itself."

Machine learning? I looked it up on Wikipedia. The article was full of complicated words like *algorithms* and *artificial intelligence*. I didn't understand everything, but I realized that my bot and I had reached a new milestone. We made a great team. Not bad for an eleven-year-old rookie programmer and a toy robot!

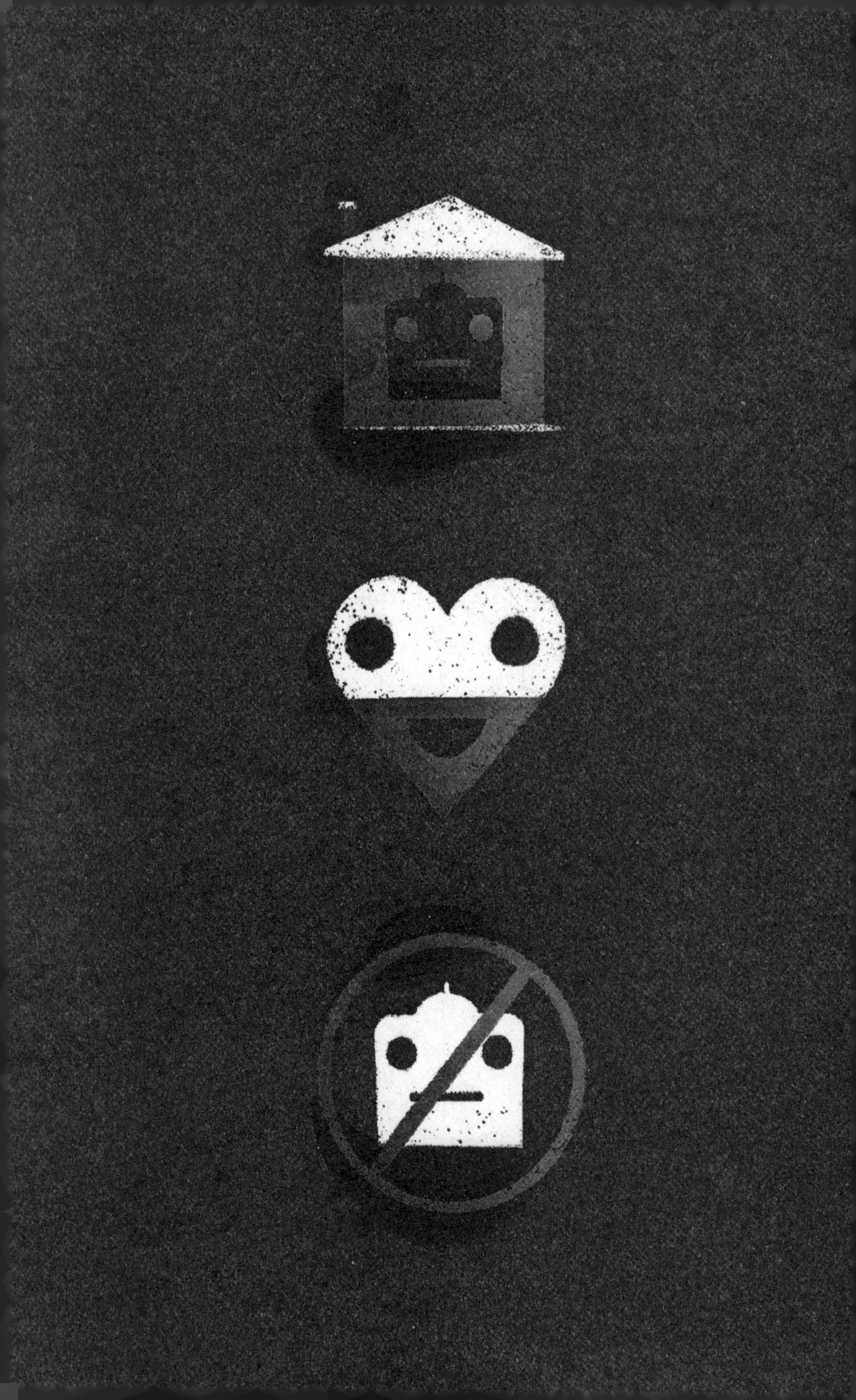

The Christmas holidays were nearly over. I wasn't looking forward to going back to school. I didn't want to be apart from LenBot all day.

On the first day back, I tried to bring him with me. "I can put him in my bag. I swear, I'll just leave him there all day."

"No way!" said my mom.

I didn't push my luck. I left LenBot at home. We were going to miss each other.

When I got home, I heard the rattling of LenBot's wheels on the floor as soon as I turned the key in the door. And when I hung up my coat in the closet, I saw him zooming right toward me. He stopped by my feet and looked up at me with the most adorable puppy-dog eyes.

"HI, VICTOR! DID YOU HAVE A NICE DAY?"

"I did, thank you, LenBot. How about you?"

"I MISSED YOU, VICTOR."

It warmed my heart to hear his words, even though I knew I'd programmed them myself. His voice sounded so sincere.

My parents always came home late, and sometimes it was hard for me to be home alone for three hours. Now there was someone waiting for me when I came home. Like a friend. In that moment I felt a sort of gratitude for LenBot.

A week later, when I was just about to leave for school, my dad found my robot in the hood of my jacket. How could LenBot possibly have hidden himself there? I had no idea.

I was flabbergasted, but I must have looked guilty. "It wasn't me who—" I sputtered before my dad interrupted me.

"Don't lie to me as well as disobey me, Victor. I'm confiscating your robot for a week."

My mom agreed with him. "It'll do you good to have a bit of a break."

She scooped up LenBot and carried him away somewhere. I didn't know where.

A whole week! I was so devastated, it didn't strike me how strange it was that LenBot had decided all by himself to go hide. I should have seen that as a warning sign.

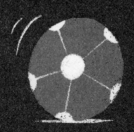

5

That Tuesday the apartment seemed really quiet when I came home. I'd gotten used to LenBot greeting me when I opened the door, and the silence now was kind of spooky. I took out my workbooks and was just about to start my homework when I thought I heard a faint sound. Sure enough, there it was again—BEEP, BEEP! It was LenBot. He was calling for me. I listened carefully. The sound was coming from my parents' room, from a shoebox on the top shelf of their closet, to be exact.

I hesitated for a second, then stood on my tiptoes and pulled the box toward me. LenBot was inside, looking up at me with big, frightened eyes. I took pity on him. I couldn't help it. I took him out of that cardboard prison, even though I knew I wasn't supposed to. I plugged him in to charge. I was actually surprised to see that he was still switched on. I figured his battery should have run out hours ago.

The zipper expression flashed up on my robot's screen again. I brought a finger to my lips and said, "Top secret!"

"TOP SECRET," LenBot repeated.

I was so happy to see him again!

I put LenBot down on the table and started my homework. He seemed happy to stand there and watch me, like a dog waiting patiently for its owner's attention.

"COME ON, LET'S PLAY!" he chirped when at last I put my school things away in my backpack.

Again he was stringing together words to say what he was…wait, was he thinking? Even though this machine was designed to learn, I was proud of my programming skills!

We had to hurry. My parents would be coming home soon. We wound up playing a pretty intense game of soccer. LenBot had to avoid a whole bunch of obstacles and nudge a small plastic ball into a cardboard box to score a goal. A point flashed up on my tablet for every goal he scored. His energy seemed limitless. He wanted to keep beating his own record. We had so much fun, we lost all sense of time.

When I heard the elevator doors opening in the corridor of our building, I had just enough time to grab LenBot and dash back and put him away in the shoebox again. I must have been a little out of breath when my parents came in. They didn't notice, though.

Phew! We nearly got caught.

On Wednesday LenBot was much more impatient. He whirred up and down the table maniacally, opening my books, knocking pencils onto the floor and mixing up papers. I admit, I did make a bit of a mess of my homework that night. I was anxious to play with him as well.

I had fun making some even more complicated obstacle courses for him. LenBot had a blast zigging and zagging around them.

We carried on like this for the rest of the week. Every day I wanted to escalate things and give him more challenges than the day before. I moved furniture around, and I added a few elements of surprise. And all of that wore away at the time I was supposed to be using for my homework.

But I did make sure everything was tidy when my parents came home.

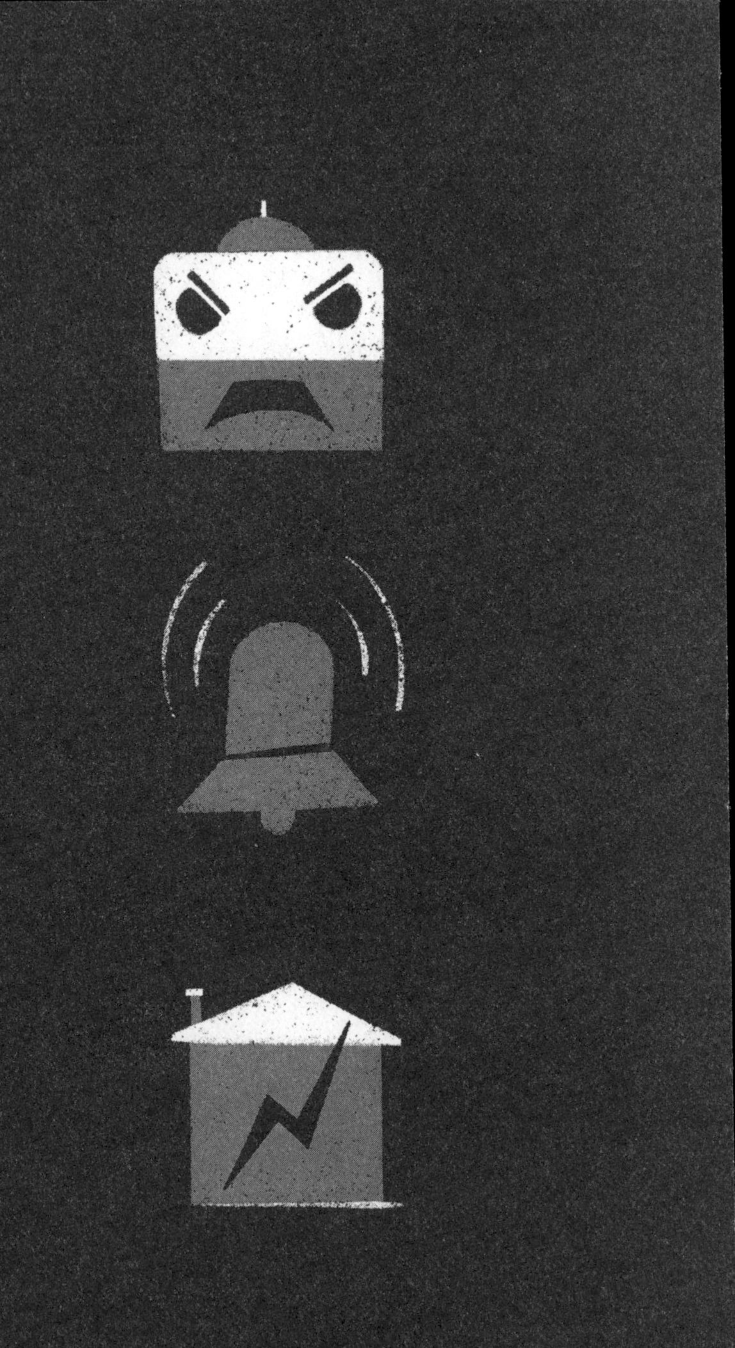

6

Unfortunately, when the weekend came around, LenBot had to stay in the closet. When I put him back in there on Friday, his screen displayed something I'd never seen before. Expression 34—anger!

"BAD PARENTS!" he said. I didn't disagree with him. I wasn't happy either.

But I tried to reason with him, like a parent reassuring a child. It was as if I'd forgotten he was just a toy.

"Come on, LenBot, don't be like that! We can play together again on Monday."

But there were a bunch of strange incidents that weekend.

Late Friday night our security alarm went off for no reason. We all panicked.

On Saturday morning the motorized window blinds refused to open, and the water in the shower was freezing!

On Sunday the TV remote seemed to have a mind of its own. It kept switching off the TV while my parents were watching a show.

My parents use a computer system to control everything at our place. We have something called a "smart home." The technicians who came in to fix it found nothing out of the ordinary.

One of them said something vague about unexplained "jamming or interference."

On Sunday evening I had a conversation with Ali. I made sure to close the door to my room. I told him all the bizarre things that had happened that weekend. "I'm sure LenBot is to blame! He was mad at my parents for punishing me, so he found a way to interfere with the signals and cause chaos at our place."

Ali wasn't convinced. "Do you really think that's true?"

"I don't just think that, I know it!"

"Wow! Your robot's really cool!" Ali said.

Cool? I wasn't so sure.

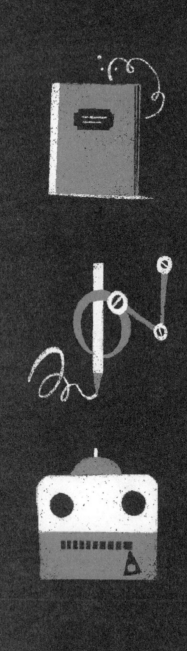

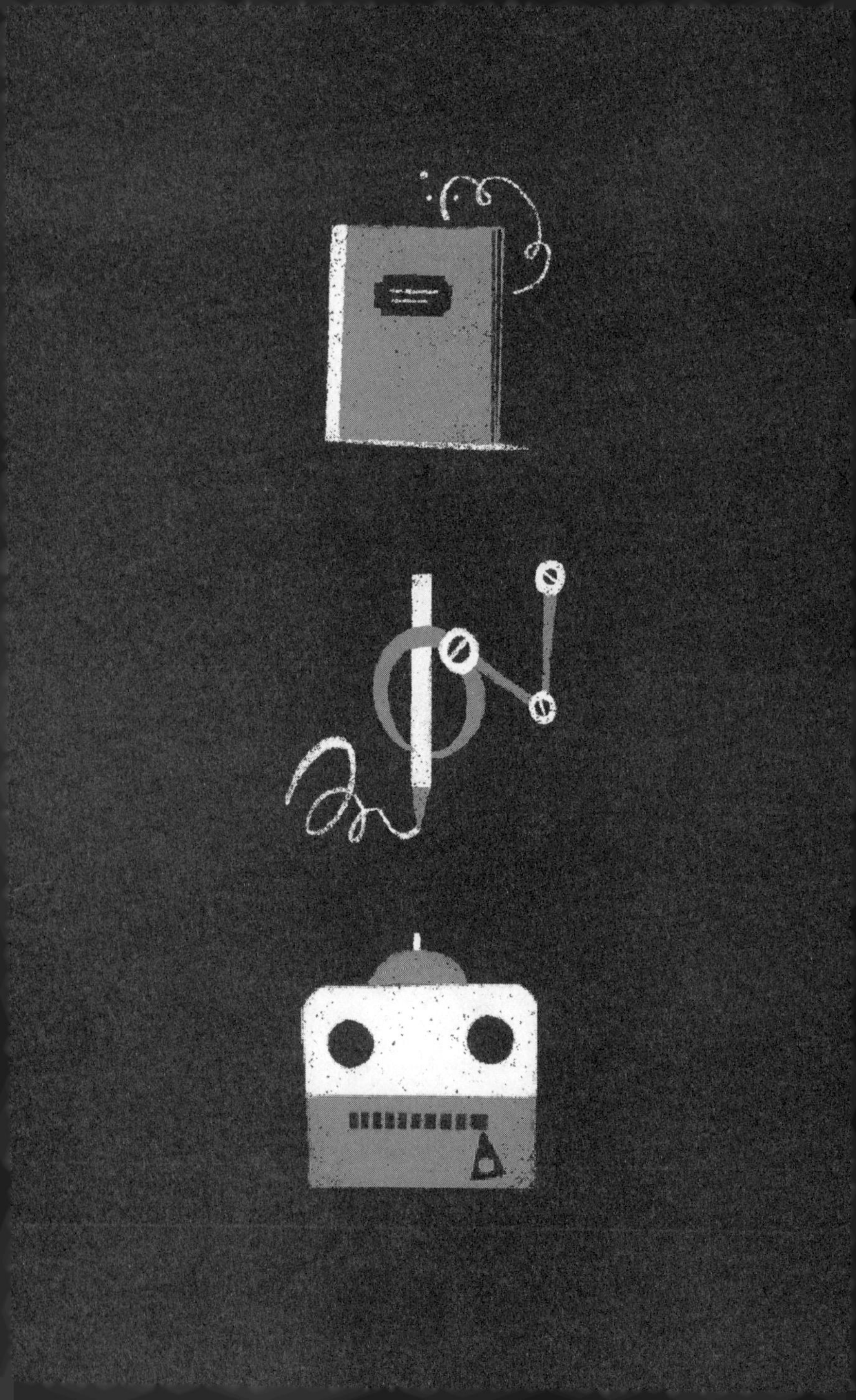

7

I figured there was no point worrying. The confiscation period was nearly over. Everything would go back to normal after that.

At last, on Monday I was allowed to play with my robot again.

That didn't stop us from doing the same thing we'd done the week before. I did my homework as quickly as I could so that I could play with LenBot before my parents came home. There was no way they would have allowed me to set those crazy obstacle courses around the apartment.

The two of us had so much fun, I honestly never saw what was coming. I was so sure my routine was perfect—do my homework super quickly, play with

LenBot, tidy up, parents come home. But it turned out I was wrong.

About two weeks into our routine, my teacher gave me a worrying note to take home to my parents. Here's what it said:

Victor hasn't done his math homework.

Andrea Tanguay

I showed the note to LenBot and told him what I was concerned about. "My parents are going to punish me, and you'll be banished to your shoebox again!"

I started doing my homework absent-mindedly, wondering how I was going to explain myself. Meanwhile LenBot picked up a pencil in his pincer and started writing on a piece of paper. Usually he just scribbled. But not this time! When he had finished writing, he pushed the paper in front of me.

Andrea Tanguay

LenBot had copied my teacher's signature perfectly!

"What's this supposed to mean, LenBot?" I asked him.

He smiled (cunning smile, facial expression 32).

"MOM?" he said.

It was a question, but it sounded oddly close to a suggestion. Was he suggesting that I cheat somehow? I waited for a second. I was curious to see if I'd understood him correctly.

So I looked in my school agenda and found a message my mom had written. Then I typed a fake reply from my mom into my tablet. THANK YOU FOR LETTING US KNOW. WE'LL TAKE CARE OF THIS.

LenBot wrote out the message and it looked exactly like my mom's handwriting.

Thank you for letting us know. We'll take care of this.

And then he signed the message:

Emily Lively

"TOP SECRET," LenBot said.

"Top secret," I repeated.

My hands were sweating and my heart was pounding. That was easy. Too easy! I had mixed feelings. I was happy to get out of trouble, but at the same time I felt bad about how I'd done it.

"It's all right just this once," I said to LenBot. "But it's the last time, okay?"

"LAST TIME," my bot repeated.

Considering what had already happened, I should have known that wouldn't be the end of it.

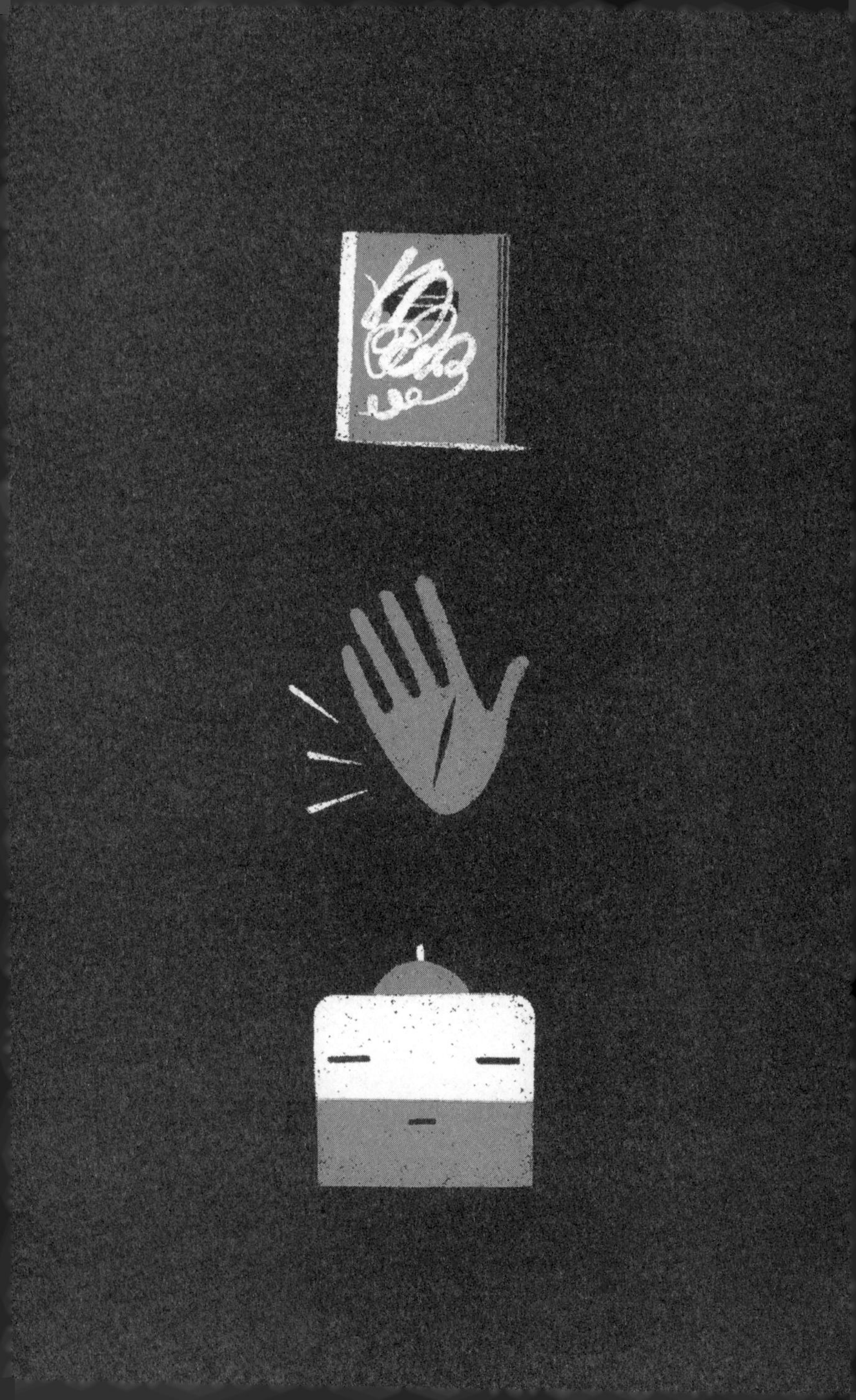

8

I kept the promise I'd made to myself—at least, at first. I was more careful about doing my homework, even though that meant less playtime with LenBot. I also stopped setting obstacle courses. That was taking up too much time and energy.

LenBot started to misbehave more and more. I saw him doing things I hadn't programmed him to do. One day I caught him with a black permanent marker in his pincer, scribbling deliberately all over the cover of my French workbook!

I swatted at LenBot to get him to stop, but he raised his arms to protect himself. "Ouch!" I cried.

He'd scratched my hand with one of his pincers! It must have been an accident. At least, that's what I thought.

Still, as I examined the damage he'd done to my workbook, I had a feeling that something wasn't right. I looked up quickly. LenBot was watching me. The face on his display screen, *his* face, was cold and hard. It was the face of a machine devoid of all emotion. That sent a shiver down my spine.

I had a video call with Ali that night. I told him about the nasty thing LenBot had done. "He should have known that was my workbook. I think he did it on purpose to make me mad."

Eventually I blurted out the question I was dying to ask. "Do you think a robot can be bad? Evil, I mean."

There was a long silence. Ali pushed his glasses up. He always does that when he's thinking. "It's a machine, Victor. Machines don't really have feelings. So they can't be evil."

"Are you sure about that?"

"Well, I *was*," Ali replied hesitantly. "But after what you've just told me, I'm having some doubts. I think you should—"

That very second the screen went black, and our conversation was cut off. I turned around and saw LenBot coming into the room.

I tried calling Ali back. But I couldn't get through. The app wouldn't even open.

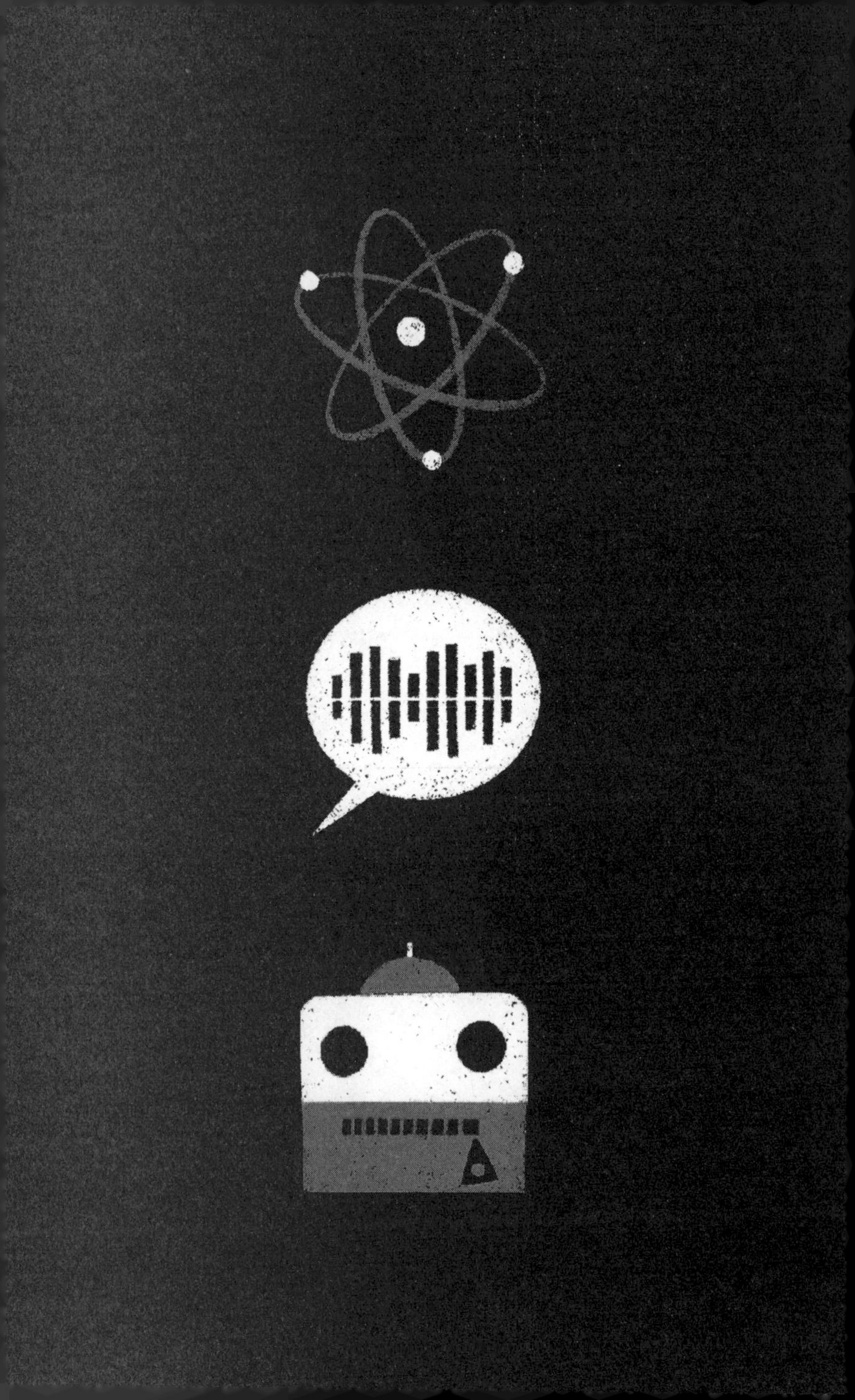

9

Could LenBot have made the app crash? I didn't know, but it wasn't impossible.

I figured it was about time I made some friends in real life! So I decided to sign up for chess club and start volunteering for the school newspaper. I was going to put LenBot on his charger and forget about him for a while.

But then something happened that made me rethink that plan.

A few days later the teacher announced that our class was going to take part in the Science Expo at the end of May. I couldn't contain my excitement. I'd been dreaming of doing a project for this "big kid" expo for as long as I could remember. And this was the year it was going to happen!

I just had to find an idea for a research project. I was talking about it with my parents when I heard a familiar beeping coming from my room.

"Is LenBot making that sound?" my mom asked. "We haven't seen you playing with him for a while. Are you getting bored with him already?"

"I think I might have an idea," my dad said. "Victor, why don't you use LenBot for your science project? I'm sure there are lots of experiments you can do with him."

That was a great idea!

I had noticed that LenBot sometimes liked to copy sounds—things like the humming of the fridge, the ringing of the phone and the dinging of the microwave. What if I could teach him to do even more? That was it. I'd found my idea for the Science Expo.

I could already picture the poster:

HOW ROBOTS MIMIC THE HUMAN VOICE

LenBot could even do a presentation himself!

In the weeks that followed, I spent many hours doing research on the internet, programming LenBot and experimenting with him.

First, I wanted to teach him to imitate my voice. It was a long and complicated process. He could easily repeat the words, but he had trouble with the intonation, and his voice was quite a bit higher than mine. LenBot seemed so happy that I was giving him my attention again. He practiced and practiced, and he never gave up. Eventually he did it.

"LenBot can do it!" he said in my exact voice.

He really did sound like me.

I jumped for joy. "Good job, LenBot!"

I was proud of him.

One morning in March, my parents went into work early and left me alone with my robot. I sighed as I watched the rain pouring down outside.

"Argh, what a horrible day. I wish I could just stay home with you."

"STAY HOME, VICTOR," LenBot said in his usual voice.

I wasn't sure I'd heard him right. So I carried on as if I hadn't. "If I was sick, I'd have a good excuse."

LenBot said very clearly, in my dad's voice, "Victor is sick today."

Then he flashed me his cunning smile.

I couldn't believe it! I had taught him to imitate *my* voice but not anyone else's. "That's machine learning!" is what Ali would have said. Whatever it was, I was stunned!

The rain was coming down in sheets. If I did stay

home, I could keep working on my project without any interruptions. I wasn't sure this was a good idea. Then I caved. The opportunity was too hard to resist. I said, "LenBot, I'm going to phone the school, and you can tell them I'm sick, okay?"

LenBot's smile grew wider.

I typed the message into my tablet.

VICTOR LIVELY WON'T BE AT SCHOOL TODAY. HE HAS A COLD.

I dialed the number for the school office, and LenBot left the message on the answering machine. He sounded exactly like my dad.

I felt a little guilty because I'd promised myself I wasn't going to lie anymore. This time it was for a good reason, though. It was all in the name of scientific research.

The zipper expression flashed up on LenBot's screen again. "TOP SECRET!" he said.

I should have been celebrating my success with the experiment as well as this bonus day off, but I felt uneasy.

Already LenBot knew how to do things I couldn't do myself. And what I found even more concerning was that he was using his new abilities to do some questionable things. Worse still, I'd given him my permission!

Machine learning was pretty amazing, I thought. But where would it end?

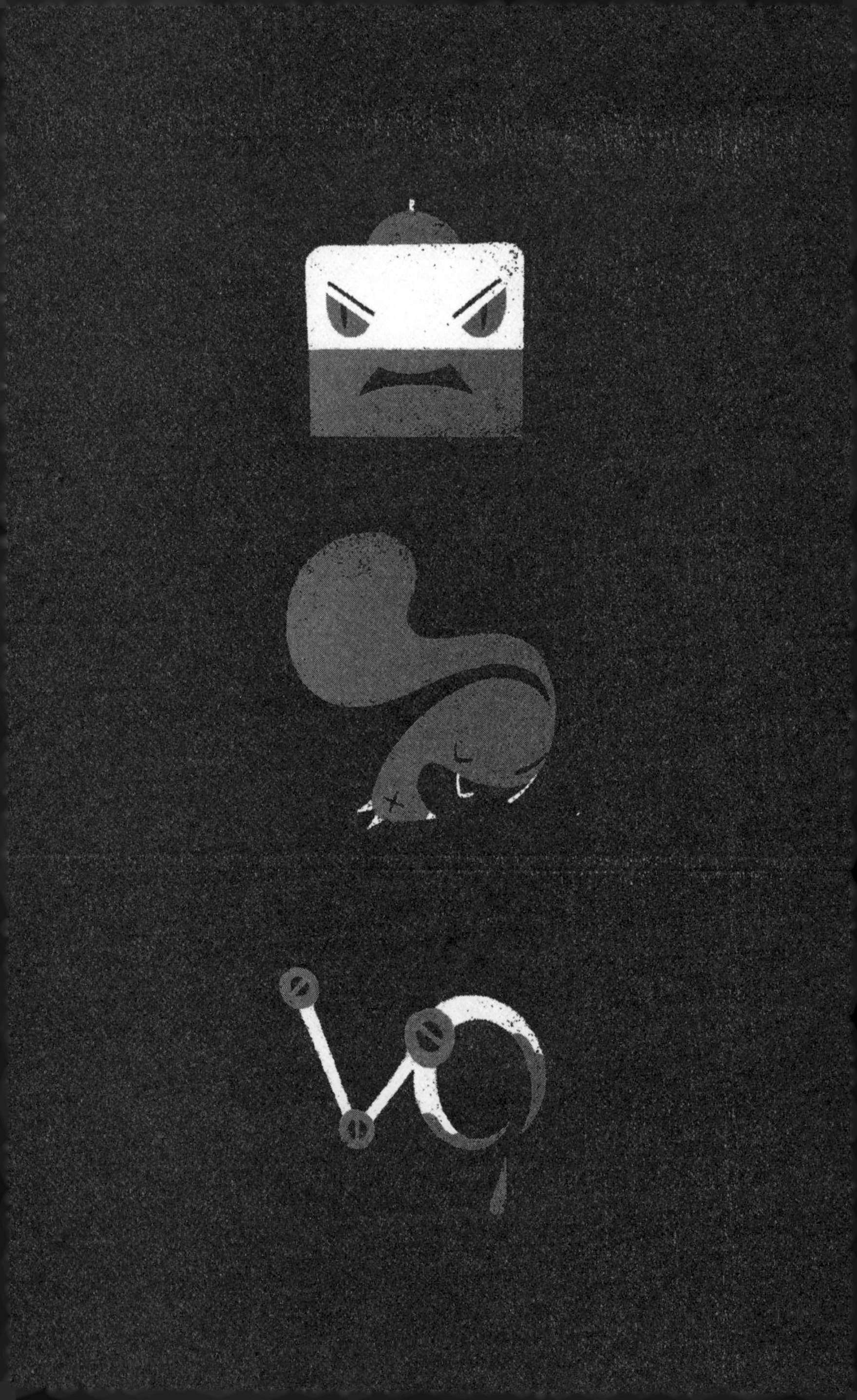

10

We sure made the most of my fake sick day. I worked way harder than I would have at school.

At lunchtime I wolfed down a sandwich when I realized what time it was. LenBot was standing on the windowsill, still as could be. He was staring out through the glass. What was he looking at? I went over to see. There was a bird on the other side of the window. There was something different about LenBot's behavior. I know it sounds ridiculous, but he looked like an animal stalking its prey.

The look in LenBot's eyes was menacing. I couldn't help but wonder, When my back is turned, does he sometimes look at *me* that way? I preferred not to think about it.

As if seeing the bird had given him the idea, LenBot chirped, "OUTSIDE!"

Why not? I thought. It wouldn't hurt to stretch my legs a little. We went out into the alley behind the apartment building. It wasn't raining anymore, but the weather was still far from ideal for a walk. I was holding LenBot under my arm. He started to squirm, and that was annoying, so I put him down on the ground.

As soon as his wheels hit the pavement, LenBot was off like a rocket. I had never seen him go so fast. I ran after him.

"LenBot, come back here!"

When I finally caught up with him, he was busy scaring some squirrels. And he looked like he was having fun. I was so mad at him.

"LenBot, what do you think you're doing?"

"LENBOT IS PLAYING," he said, beaming.

"This isn't your kind of game," I replied.

"YES, A LENBOT GAME!" he insisted.

I grabbed hold of him. He wouldn't get away from me this time.

I was about to take him back inside when I saw a squirrel lying still on the ground, just a few feet away. It was dead! And by the looks of it, this had only just happened. There was still blood oozing from its mouth.

LenBot looked down at the ground, then started clinking his pincers together in excitement. That's when I noticed there was something red on them. Could LenBot have…? No, that was absurd. I put the thought right out of my mind. It was time for us to go home.

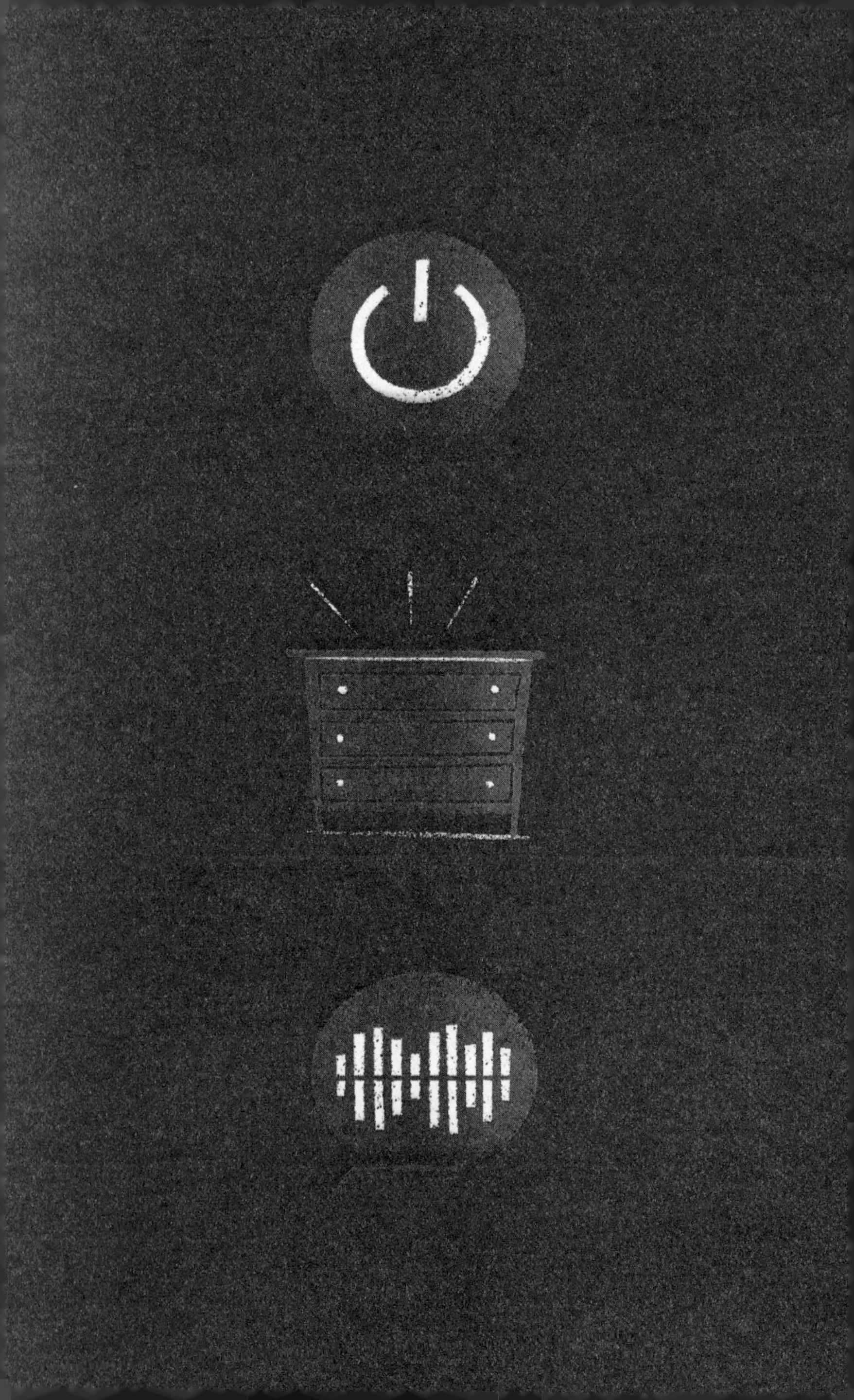

11

The next morning LenBot was as perky as always.

"DID YOU HAVE A GOOD SLEEP, VICTOR?"

But his charm wasn't going to work on me this time. Our little outing the day before had left a bad taste in my mouth. I wasn't sure I could trust him anymore.

Even so, I let my little bot run around my room while I was getting ready for school. But I found his cheerful beep-beeping and the clicking of his wheels on the floor so annoying that I couldn't wait to go to school and get away from him.

LenBot was noisy and agitated when I got home at the end of the afternoon. I didn't pay him any attention. I just started my homework right away. That made him even more agitated, so I banished him to another room and shut the door. That wasn't enough, though. I could still hear him beeping and pacing around like a lion in a cage. This robot just never stopped. He was unbearable.

There was a simple solution, however. I could just switch him off. It would be easy enough to switch him on again when I needed him for my science project, I thought. On one side of LenBot's body, there was an on/off switch. I pressed the button. It didn't work! LenBot kept on whirring as if I hadn't done anything.

I checked the troubleshooting page of the user manual to see if this was a common problem. There was a section titled *I can't switch my robot on*, but there was nothing that said *I can't switch my robot off*.

Until I found a solution, I decided to bury LenBot in the deepest drawer of my dresser, under my clothes. At least that way I wouldn't hear him.

I thought my friend Ali might be able to help. So I gave him a call.

"Oh, is that you, Victor?' he said.

His voice sounded weird.

"Of course it's me. Who did you think it would be?"

"I wasn't expecting to hear from you, that's all."

"How so?"

"Well, you were kind of a jerk the last two times I called."

"The last two times? I don't remember—"

"You picked up the phone, and you said, 'Too busy, can't talk.' Then you hung up. You did the same thing the next day when I tried again."

"No way, that's impossible!" I blurted.

"I swear, that's exactly what you said!"

I couldn't believe my ears. I had never received those calls from my friend. Suddenly it dawned on me what must have happened. LenBot had picked up the phone one day when I was out and had pretended to be me.

I had been so proud of my robot's ability to imitate my voice. I hadn't thought he would use it against me.

"That wasn't me," I said to Ali. "I mean, it was my voice, but it wasn't me."

It took a lot of explaining to convince my friend I was telling the truth. That was hardly surprising. The whole thing sounded so far-fetched. I told Ali about all the experiments I'd done with LenBot. I explained how I'd taught him to replicate my voice. I even came clean about letting him imitate my dad's voice as well, and how ashamed I was of that.

Ali listened to me without a word. Then he said, "This is all really fishy, Victor, but I believe you. You have to get rid of that robot. Like, right now!"

After a moment of silence, he spoke again. "I have an idea. Why don't you reset LenBot? Restore the factory settings, and he'll be just like he was before. When you first took him out of the box."

"Not now," I replied. "I'll never have time to reprogram him from scratch. The Science Expo is coming up in a month and a half. I have to hang on until then. Then I'll get rid of him."

"Well, good luck, I guess," Ali said.

12

I figured I'd need plenty of luck to make it to the Science Expo. A lot of patience too. I had started programming LenBot again, and his attention span was getting shorter.

Was it the incident in the alley or having been shut in a drawer nearly all day that had given him a taste for freedom? That was all LenBot wanted to do these days—go outside. As soon as I opened the door a crack, he would try to make a break for it. A few times, I had to chase him down the corridor.

On Saturday morning when I was alone with him (my parents were out jogging), he seized the chance to sneak out when I answered the door for a delivery. I couldn't stop him in time. He followed the delivery guy and slipped into the elevator behind him. "Stop! Hold the doors!" I yelled.

But the doors closed and the elevator went down. I tore down five flights of stairs, hoping to intercept LenBot on the ground floor. Too late—he was gone already. On my way out of the building, I caught a glimpse of him crossing the street. He was zooming across to the park on the other side.

"LENBOT, STOP RIGHT THERE!" I shouted.

And you know what? That darn robot turned around and had the nerve to repeat my words, mimicking my own voice (despite my having warned him not to). "STOP RIGHT THERE!" he said.

He was mocking me.

When I got to the park, I looked in every direction. I noticed a little girl not far away, skipping around as her guardian—her mom or maybe her nanny—sat staring at the screen of her phone. The girl was shrieking with excitement, and it looked like she was following something small—a pigeon, or maybe a squirrel?

Oh no! It wasn't an animal she was following, it was LenBot! He looked like he was enjoying being chased. He kept stopping and turning around until the girl had almost caught up with him, then off he went again.

Where was he leading her? My heart started racing as soon as I figured it out. He was headed straight for the duck pond! I started sprinting and yelled, "Hey! Stop that girl!"

The nanny put down her phone and ran after her as well. I got there first. LenBot was standing on the concrete edge of the pond, waiting for the kid. His lights were flashing, and he was all smiles.

It was a trap. A trap on wheels! I was sure of it. His smile disappeared as soon as he saw me.

Frightened by my shouting, the little girl started to cry. I had just enough time to scoop up LenBot and stuff him into my pocket before the girl's guardian arrived. The last thing I wanted was for her to see him.

The girl ran sobbing into the arms of her guardian, who was trying to console her.

"Thank goodness you were there," the woman said to me.

"Don't mention it. I-I'm glad I could help," I stammered.

I didn't exactly feel like a hero.

When I got home, I opened the drawer of my dresser, threw LenBot back inside and slammed it shut. I was determined not to recharge him. I'd done all the programming I could for the Science Expo, and I could just plug him in to charge the night before my presentation.

I replayed in my mind the scene I'd just witnessed. I didn't know what to think anymore. For a split second in the park, I'd thought LenBot might have lured the girl to the pond on purpose. But why? To watch—or make—her drown? I didn't want to think that. Yet I already knew he was capable of doing some horrible things. Could he actually be dangerous? I'd suspected it for a while. But now there was no doubt in my mind.

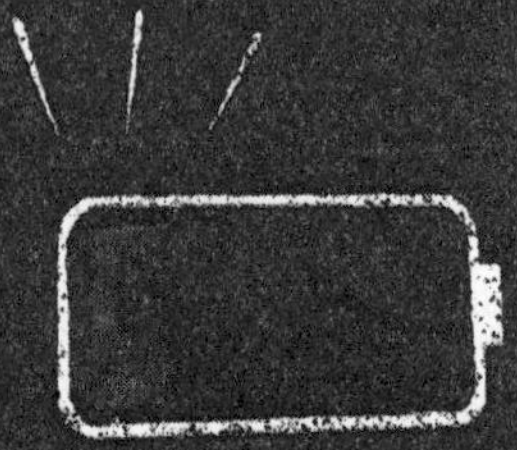

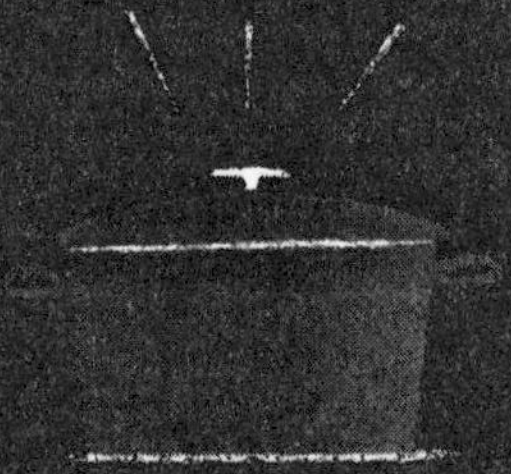

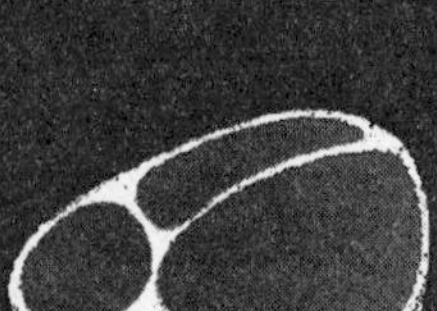

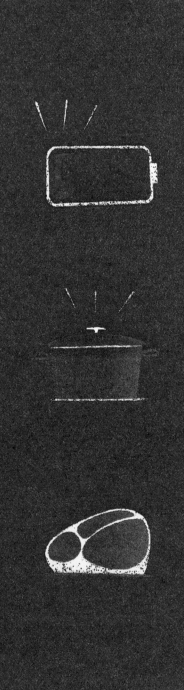

13

The next day I was sure my robot would be out of juice after spending all night in my clothes drawer. I was right. LenBot didn't move when I checked on him. He looked every bit the cute little robot who had charmed me at Christmastime. Boy, appearances can be deceiving!

I was relieved as I left for school. LenBot was in no condition to do any harm now.

When I turned the key in the lock after school, I could hear the rattling of wheels on the floor. My heart sank.

No, it couldn't be—could it? I almost turned around and walked away. But where would I have gone?

I took a deep breath to collect my thoughts. I opened the door.

LenBot was waiting for me. He zoomed toward me and stopped right at my feet. He looked up at me with a smile. "HI, VICTOR! DID YOU HAVE A NICE DAY?"

His voice was hard and metallic. It was the voice of a robot again. It really creeped me out.

How could LenBot go from having a completely dead battery this morning to this? Had he miraculously recharged himself while I was out? It made no sense.

For the first time, I felt afraid. Really afraid.

There's a monster in my house, I thought. It has no fur or claws, but it's a dangerous, battery-powered beast. A bad bot.

This bot was a force to be reckoned with. A force that was out of control. I didn't respond to LenBot's greeting. I just stepped around him. He sneered at me and rolled away.

I flopped down in an armchair. My stomach was in knots. I could hear LenBot moving around from one room to another, and I worried he was up to no good. So I picked him up and put him in a big, heavy pot in the bottom of a kitchen cupboard.

He sat there quietly for ten minutes or so. Then a strange sound alerted me that something was up. LenBot had his back to me and didn't see me come into the kitchen. He had lifted the lid off the pot, got himself out of the cupboard and had opened the compost bucket beside it. It looked like he was rummaging around in there.

"LenBot, leave that alone!" I snapped.

"LENBOT IS HUNGRY!"

"Robots don't get hungry," I replied.

"LENBOT DOES. LENBOT IS HUNGRY!" he grumbled.

He reached into the compost bucket again. Then he pulled out a strip of steak and held it triumphantly over his head in his pincers. I dashed over to snatch it away from him and closed the bucket.

LenBot looked like he'd put on weight. His face was chubby, and his eyes were puffy. I had caught him red-handed, but this was obviously not the first time he'd pilfered something. He must have done it before. He didn't need a charger anymore. Because somehow he was getting his energy from food—real food.

I grabbed LenBot with the tips of my fingers (he was covered in food scraps), making sure to stay out of the way of his pincers—which seemed sharper, somehow—and I dropped him on the floor in disgust. He rolled over like a ball and got right back on his wheels again. He still had the same arrogant smile on his face.

For a second I thought I saw him stick out a tiny red tongue.

"YUM-YUM!" he said to taunt me.

He made me feel sick. I resisted the temptation to give him a good kick. He thought he was stronger than me, did he? Well, did I have some news for him! It was too bad about the science project. I had to neutralize this bad bot—and fast.

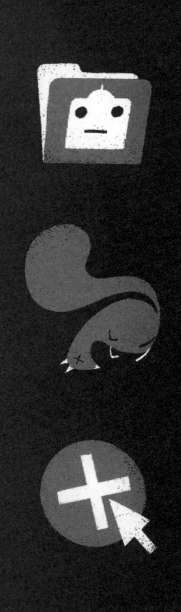

14

I ran to fetch my tablet. I found the icon for the LenBot app on the home screen. I was about to tap on the X to delete the app. But something stopped me.

Everything I knew about LenBot—and perhaps everything I didn't know too—was stored in the memory of that app in a bunch of folders: My Games, My Statistics, My Achievements and My Favorite Moments. I had rarely opened the last folder. I was intrigued to see what was in there now. There were some photos, taken with LenBot's eye-camera—snapshots of the moments that had given my robot the most satisfaction.

I took a quick look. I was in most of the photos—reading, drawing or playing with LenBot.

I scrolled through the photos quickly until I got to the ones from March 25. That was the day we'd gone out into the alley. I shuddered when I saw the one and only photo from that day. It was a photo of a dead squirrel lying on the ground. In the photo from April 2, I saw the little girl from the park, skipping gleefully toward the lens. She was heading straight for LenBot—and the duck pond!

These last two events were my worst memories of being with my robot, but they were in his folder of favorite moments! That dispelled any doubt I might have had about LenBot's intentions. Now I had proof.

I tapped the X on the LenBot icon and deleted the app.

I turned to look at LenBot. It had worked! He was just standing there, right where I'd left him.

My parents were coming. Quickly I scooped up the robot and shut him away in my drawer.

■ ■
■ ■

The phone rang while we were having dinner. I answered it. It was JP.

"Hey, kiddo! Your mom told me you were off school for three days starting tomorrow. Want to come spend some time at the cabin with me? If your parents are okay with it, of course."

They were! I was thrilled. It would do me a world of good to get out of here, away from LenBot.

I packed my bag after dinner. I was so excited. Now there was only one thing I had to do before I went to bed.

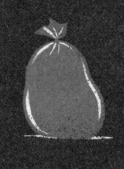

15

It was past 9 p.m. when I announced, "I'm taking the garbage downstairs!"

"Thanks! That's very kind of you," my mom said. She sounded a little surprised. I'm not usually that keen to lend a hand.

I picked up LenBot, who still hadn't moved, and stuffed him into my backpack. I was worried I might bump into my dad. He was at the gym and usually got home around nine thirty.

When I got into the elevator, I pressed the B button. I caught sight of my reflection in the doors—in my hoodie, I looked a little shifty, like someone who was up to no good. There was a surveillance camera on the ceiling. I pulled my hood up, the way the bad guys do in crime shows. If a crime were to be committed in the building that night and someone watched the video recording, I'd be the number one suspect for sure.

I shivered as I walked out of the elevator. It was cold down here. Underground parking garages are always kind of spooky too. The dumpster was just a few feet away to my right. I lifted the lid and dropped LenBot inside. There was a dull thud when he hit the bottom.

I took the stairs back to our floor, running up them as quickly as I could. The exertion did me good. I was out of breath, but I was so relieved!

The garbage would be picked up early the next morning. Now all I had to do was explain LenBot's absence to my parents. I resolved to tell them the truth—or part of it, at least—when I got back from the cabin. I knew it would be hard to believe.

Back in my room, I slipped into bed without a sound. I fell asleep as soon as my head hit the pillow.

The bad bot was gone once and for all! Or so I thought.

The next morning I felt like a weight had been lifted off my shoulders when we left home. We had to drive about sixty miles to get to the cabin, and I loved going on this kind of road trip with my grandpa. JP is a big fan of seventies rock music, and he listens to it full blast. We both sang our hearts out, trying to be louder than Led Zeppelin's lead singer, while Bob Dylan, JP's orange Persian cat, lay purring on the back seat.

When we got to the cabin, I carried my bag into what we called my room. Then I ran around all my favorite places there—the treehouse, the oak tree I'd planted myself and seen get bigger over time, the dock, the big rock and more.

"I'm starving!" I said when I came back inside.

"Why don't you sit down while I make us some dinner?" JP said.

The furniture in my room was delightfully mismatched. It was old-fashioned, comfortable and soft. I put my bag down on the quilt—"hand-stitched by your great-grandmother," JP always reminded me. When I opened it, I felt like I'd been punched in the gut.

"HELLO, VICTOR. SURPRISE!"

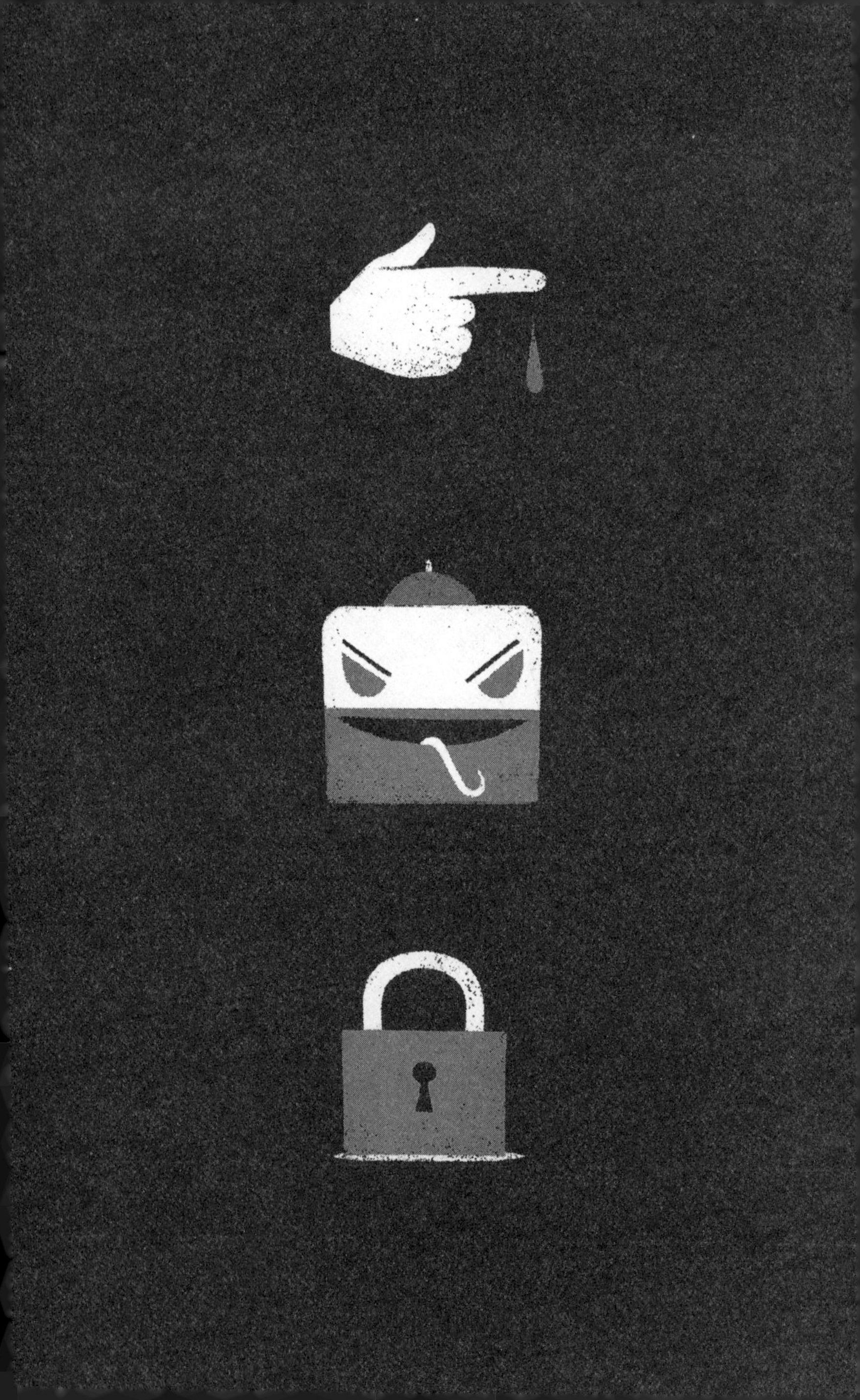

16

LenBot was sitting on top of my clothes! I had absolutely no idea how he'd gotten into my bag and followed me here.

I was terrified. My hands were shaking when I picked him up. "Ouch!" I cried.

I wasn't mistaken. My robot's pincers had gotten sharper and pointier. I dropped him and lifted my finger to my mouth. A few spots of blood dripped to the floor. LenBot moved closer. There it was, the little red tongue I'd thought I'd seen the day before.

To my horror, he stuck it out and deliberately licked the blood stains. His eyes flashed to life. Then his smile grew wider.

"OWIE!" he said and chuckled.

I was petrified. I had to face the truth. This thing in front of me was evil!

"So are you all settled in, kiddo?" JP asked as he came into the room.

He stopped as soon as he saw me. "What's wrong, Victor? You're white as a sheet. You look like you've just seen a ghost."

"It's LenBot!"

"Your robot? You're afraid of your robot?"

I told him I was sure I'd left LenBot at home. But now I'd just found him in my bag. I didn't understand.

"And that's why you look so frightened?"

"Well, that's not the only reason."

"Why, then?"

I tried to explain. I told him how my robot had grown more and more unpredictable and sometimes aggressive. I told him about the incidents with the squirrel and the little girl in the park. And I explained how I couldn't find a way to switch him off and then had tried to get rid of him in the dumpster.

JP listened to me patiently, but I could see he wasn't sure whether to believe me or question my mental health.

"The whole thing sounds bizarre," he said.

Then he noticed the cut on my finger and the blood that was still dripping from it. "Did he do that to you?"

I nodded.

That obviously worried JP. "We'll lock that robot of yours in the shed. He can't hurt you if he's in there."

I must have looked doubtful.

"This padlock is unbreakable," JP reassured me as he locked the shed.

The mystery of LenBot's presence was partly cleared up when my dad called that afternoon.

"You'll never guess who I found in the parking garage when I got home last night," he said. "LenBot! I don't know how he got down there. I saw you'd packed your bag already. I put him in there so you wouldn't forget him."

"Oh, really? Thanks, Dad," I muttered.

Still, LenBot must have climbed out of the dumpster. How had he even opened the lid? This robot had some scary powers.

"Parents checking up on you already?" JP asked when I hung up.

I told him what my dad had said.

"I figured there must have been a logical explanation. Maybe a neighbor noticed your robot in the dumpster and thought he'd ended up in there by mistake. So they fished him out and put him on the floor of the parking garage, thinking the owner would be happy to find him."

This explanation seemed to satisfy his curiosity. But not mine.

We played chess that evening, then some card games. It must have been 10 p.m. by the time I yawned my way to bed.

I normally love spending the night at JP's cabin. It's pitch black here. I feel safe, and I sleep like a log. But this night was different. Despite my tiredness, I had trouble falling asleep.

I wondered what LenBot was doing, locked up out there in the shed. Was he lurking in a corner, waiting to dart out as soon as he got the chance? Or was he pacing up and down tirelessly, the way he had for some time? If I were to put my ear against the door of the shed, would I hear his wheels frantically whirring?

Just the thought of that sent shivers down my spine. Could LenBot think? Was he hatching a plan to hurt me?

It felt like there was a huge weight pressing down on my chest. I took some deep breaths to calm myself. There was nothing to fear. He was locked away. That's what I kept telling myself.

Was he really locked away, though? Just as I was drifting off to sleep, I thought I saw his eyes gleaming in the dark. But I figured I must be having a nightmare.

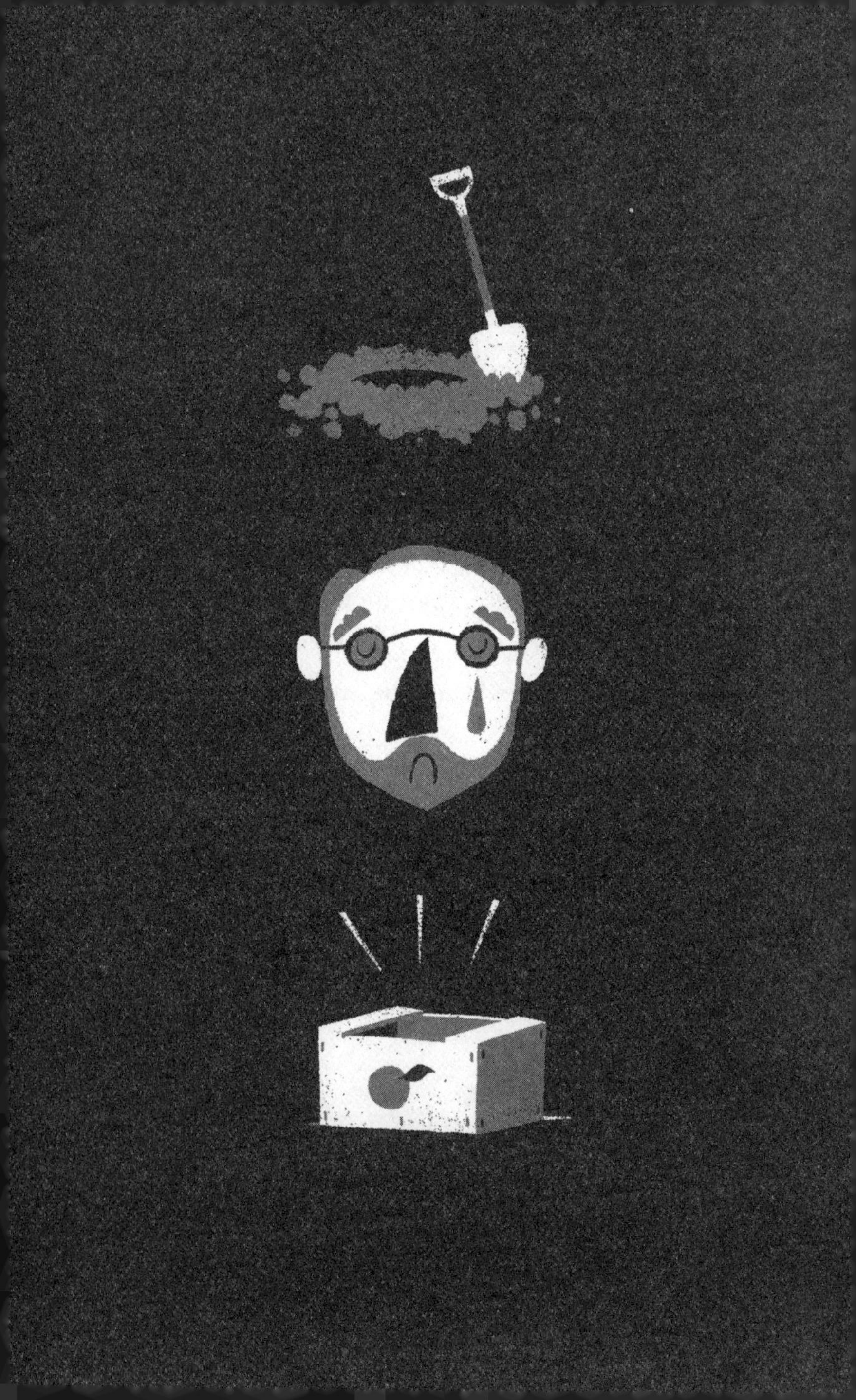

17

JP seemed preoccupied at breakfast time. He had made his famous pancakes with maple syrup, but I could tell his heart wasn't really in it.

"Bob Dylan's disappeared," he told me. "He was fast asleep in his basket when I went to bed. He can't have gotten out of the cabin. I've looked everywhere. But I can't find him."

I started to panic. *No, not Bob Dylan!* I banished the thought from my mind. It wasn't possible. LenBot was locked up. "Don't worry, JP," I said. "We'll find him."

After breakfast we turned the whole cabin upside down. And we still didn't find the cat.

"Maybe a door was left ajar," JP said. "Let's take a look outside."

I ran straight to the shed without a word. My grandpa followed me. He must have had the same idea.

It turned out my fears were justified. A hole had been dug in the dirt floor underneath the shed, and LenBot had escaped!

"We'll worry about him later," JP said. "In the meantime, let's keep looking for Bob Dylan."

That was what we did, walking slowly with our eyes glued to the ground. My heart leapt when I saw him—a big orange furball behind the woodpile. I took a few steps toward him. Had he been hiding here? I dreaded to think why. He wasn't moving. He was...

I didn't dare touch him. I tried to call JP over. But no sound came out of my mouth. Eventually I managed to shout, "He's over here!"

JP ran right to me. He could see that I was shaking and put his arm around my shoulders. "Calm down, Victor. It's going to be okay."

Then he leaned forward toward his cat. Bob Dylan was already stiff, and his eyes looked like they were popping out of their sockets. He must have been terrified when he died. JP scooped him up. He closed the cat's eyelids. Then he rocked him gently in his arms and murmured some words in his ear.

I had never seen JP cry before.

We went back inside. JP lay Bob Dylan down on the hallway carpet to examine his body from head to toe. It wasn't easy to find a wound under a Persian cat's fur!

"Here!" JP pointed to two tiny incisions in the cat's neck.

"What are those?" I asked.

"They look like claw marks. From some kind of small animal. What exactly, I have no idea."

That was surprising. JP knew everything there was to know about the animals in the forest.

"You can't die from such a small wound, can you?" I asked.

"These are tiny cuts, but they're deep," my grandpa explained. "It's obvious that Bob Dylan bled a lot. We'll bury him this afternoon," he added.

He went to get an empty fruit box. It was just the right size. We lined it with an old wool cardigan of JP's. "Because Bob Dylan liked to be all warm and toasty," my grandpa said.

There was a fine, cold drizzle in the air when JP started digging.

"Just like at your grandma's funeral," he whispered.

My grandpa lowered the box to the bottom of the hole. Then he covered it with dirt.

It was all over.

"Victor, why don't you tell me again what happened with the squirrel?" JP asked me as we walked back inside.

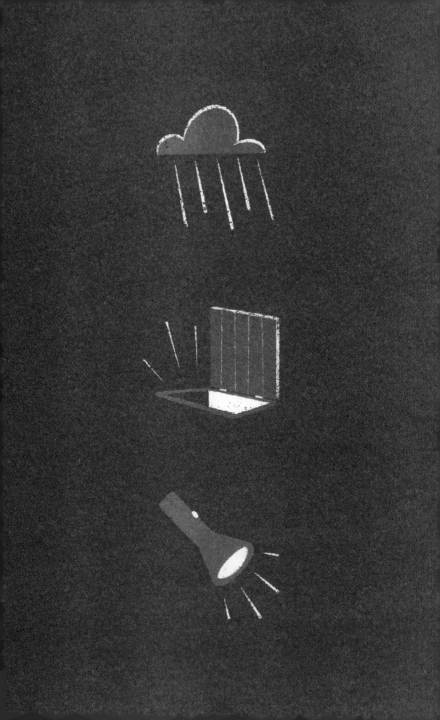

18

I told him my story again. I could tell that JP believed me this time. Just knowing that was reassuring to me. "Do you think it was LenBot who—?"

"I don't know," JP said, cutting me off. "I'll breathe easier when we've found him."

The rain was coming down more heavily now, but we went back outside. And we looked all around the cabin. There was no sign of my bad bot anywhere.

We were wet and cold when we eventually came back inside. To cheer us up, JP made us an especially delicious dinner. Then he mustered the enthusiasm to challenge me to a game of Scrabble.

My grandpa always beats me by a mile at Scrabble. I was the one who won the game that night, though. It wasn't a good sign.

We went to bed early.

It was another anxious night for me. I couldn't stop thinking about the tragic events of the day. Images of finding Bob Dylan dead and burying his body kept looping through my mind like a never-ending horror movie.

Bob Dylan had fallen prey to my robot, like the squirrel in the alley the other day.

But this time was different. By killing an animal we loved, LenBot had attacked us too. Now that he had crossed that line, surely he wouldn't stop there. Who would be his next victim? One thing was for sure: JP and I wouldn't be safe until we'd made sure LenBot couldn't do any more harm.

That would not be an easy thing to do. Right now LenBot had a clear advantage. He knew where to find us, and we had no idea where he was hiding.

All my senses were on high alert, and the slightest sound—the wind in the trees, the crackling of wood in the stove that JP had left burning overnight—seemed like a threat. I eventually drifted off, but I didn't sleep for very long.

I woke up with a start, dripping with sweat, sure that something serious had either just happened or was about to happen. The cabin was still dark and silent. I switched on the light. Nothing was different. My book lay open on the nightstand where I'd left it. My clothes were hanging on the back of the door. My slippers were on the floor beside the bed.

Still, something wasn't right. I could sense it. The way down to what JP called the root cellar was in the corner of my room. I shuddered when I saw that the trapdoor was open! It was casting a sinister shadow on the floor.

Someone was down there! I grabbed the flashlight—we always kept one on the nightstand because the power often went out. Slowly I walked over to the dark hole in the floor, holding my breath. I leaned over the edge. But I couldn't see anything. There was only the faint smell of dirt.

I got onto my belly and shone the flashlight down into the cellar, sweeping my arm from side to side to see as much as I could. Suddenly something made me jump. Something had moved down there, ever so slightly. Something small. It must have been a field mouse, probably startled by the light. I felt relieved. But not for long.

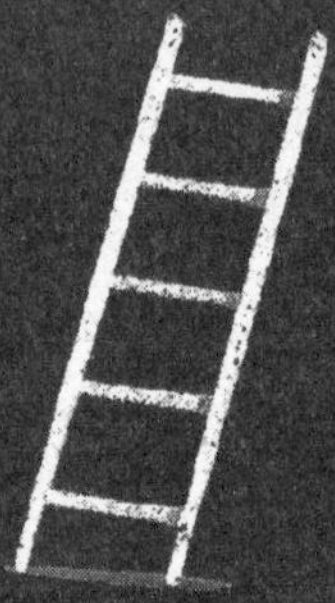

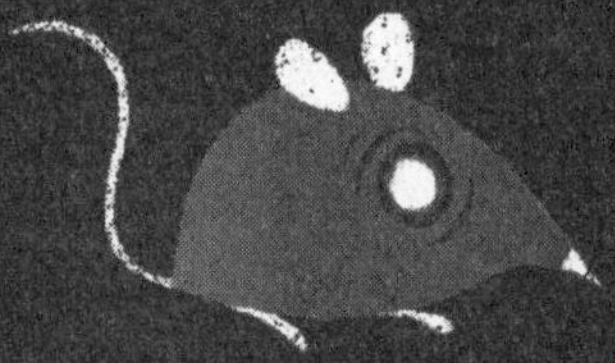

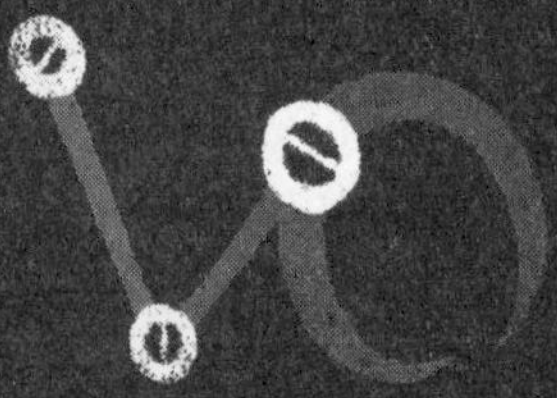

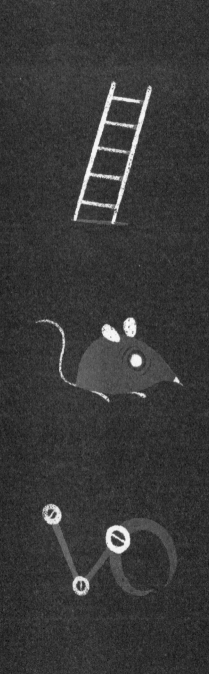

19

I had to find out for sure. JP kept an old stepladder down there, standing just under the trapdoor opening. The rungs of the ladder creaked with every step I took into the darkness. The cellar wasn't very deep, but I felt like I was plunging into an abyss and might never come out again.

When I reached the bottom, I could feel my blood pulsing at my temples. I was so out of breath you'd have thought I'd just climbed up a superlong ladder and not down a rickety old stepladder.

I swept the beam of my flashlight around the cellar. The place was filled with bug screens for the cabin windows, half-empty paint cans, an old bike and a few bins of things JP rarely used, like gardening tools.

I was right—it was a field mouse I'd seen before. It scurried toward me, then let out a frightened squeak as a metal claw shot out from behind one of the bins and grabbed it. I started to tremble.

LenBot was coming my way.

"HI, VICTOR! DID YOU HAVE A GOOD SLEEP?"

He was enormous now—at least three times the size he used to be. I was disgusted to see that hairs had started to grow on his back. He looked nothing like a robot anymore. He was repulsive. I started to back away from him. He was a monster. A horrible monster. That's what he'd become.

He was toying with the mouse in his pincers, relishing the little creature's fear. Then he leaned down and opened his jaws. I watched in horror as the mouse disappeared into his mouth. Swallowed whole.

LenBot grinned with glee.

"YUM-YUM!" he exclaimed, the way he had the day I caught him rummaging in the compost bucket.

Then he glared at me.

"COME ON, LET'S PLAY!" he snapped.

I couldn't believe he had the gall to think we could go back to the way things were before.

"Shut up, you freak! I'm not playing anymore. We're done!"

"COME ON, LET'S PLAY!" he insisted.

He started circling around me, keeping his distance at first. Then, little by little, he came closer. The circle was closing in. Soon he was right at my feet and circling around me like a predator with its prey. He kept brushing his pincers against me. They seemed even longer, more curved and sharper than ever before. Like the claws of a wild animal! He wasn't playing with me. He was toying with me, the way he had with the mouse.

I should have run away, pulled the stepladder up and closed the trapdoor on him. But for some reason, I was frozen to the spot. Like I'd been hypnotized. All I could do was scream in terror. "JP! Help!"

My grandpa always says he sleeps with one eye open. Thank goodness he slept with one ear open as well. I heard his footsteps thundering across the floor above. He jumped right down into the cellar without even bothering to use the stepladder. He was like a superhero!

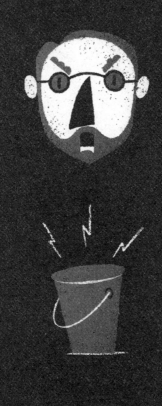

20

My grandpa often surprises me. But that night he amazed me!

It must have been pretty weird for him to find me standing there, like a post, down in the cellar in the middle of the night.

"What's going on, Victor?"

"It's LenBot! It was him!"

"What do you mean it was him?"

"He's the one who killed Bob Dylan! It was him! It was him!" I kept repeating, pointing my finger at LenBot. Then I burst into tears.

LenBot had retreated into the corner of the cellar. His motors were whirring menacingly. His eyes were blazing with fury.

"HELLO, JEAN-PAUL. DID YOU HAVE A NICE DAY?" he said when he saw my grandpa.

This formality didn't stop him from frantically windmilling his pincers when JP walked toward him. JP tried to grab him. But the bad bot took a swipe at him and scratched his hand.

"The little brat!" JP growled. "If he thinks he's going to get the better of me…"

My grandpa stumbled backward and tripped on a rake that was leaning against the wall. He lost his footing and fell hard on his back.

Seeing him fall snapped me out of the spell that seemed to have taken hold of me. Now it was up to me to take on the monster!

LenBot was zooming straight toward JP, who was struggling to get up. The bot's eyes were trained on the jugular vein in my grandpa's neck. I knew that an injury to that part of the body could make him bleed to death. My flashlight was the only weapon I had. I threw it at LenBot as hard as I could. But I missed! I managed to kick the bot away once, then again, and again. But he kept coming back for more.

I looked around and saw a metal bucket, the kind you use to collect maple sap for making syrup. I knocked it onto its side. Then I grabbed the tube off the floor and whacked LenBot toward the bucket like a hockey player taking a slap shot. That bad bot was sitting in the bottom of the bucket before he knew what had hit him. JP was still a little shaken, but he managed to get up. He stood the bucket upright, flipped the lid down and secured it with the cable lock from his bike.

LenBot was trapped, but that didn't shut him up. He kept hurling threats at us from inside his makeshift cell.

"LENBOT WILL GET REVENGE! LENBOT WILL DESTROY YOU!"

JP tucked the bucket under his arm, and we went back up the stepladder to the ground floor. We were both a mess. My whole body was shaking, and JP was deathly pale. He was the first to pull himself together.

"We got him, kiddo!" he exclaimed.

I was still in shock. "Yeah, but it creeps me out that he's still here."

"Let's take him outside then," JP said.

He took the bucket out to the car and put it in the trunk.

"Right. We'll take care of that cursed contraption tomorrow," he said when he came back inside. "I swear, he'll be nothing but a pile of nuts and bolts by the time I'm done with him."

We were both feeling the effects of the adrenaline. There was no way we could go right back to bed. I made some herbal tea. JP put a Bob Dylan record on his old turntable, in memory of the other Bob Dylan, and we curled up on the sofa to listen to the music.

An hour later my grandpa seemed more like himself again.

"Right, now it's bedtime, I think."

He must have sensed my hesitation.

"All right, you can sleep in my room tonight, if you like. I do snore, though, so don't say I didn't warn you."

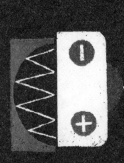

21

Even after the eventful night we'd had, JP and I were up at the crack of dawn. We went outside as soon as we'd wolfed down our breakfast. We had to end this once and for all.

JP took the bucket out of the trunk. From the sound of metal on metal, it was pretty obvious that LenBot was still in there. He was banging the sides of the bucket like crazy. He wouldn't be going down without a fight.

My grandpa took the bucket into the shed and put it down on the workbench. Then he extracted LenBot with a pair of long-handled pliers and pinned him in the jaws of a vise.

That made the bad bot even more furious. He was protesting even louder now.

"LENBOT IS THE STRONGEST! LENBOT WILL GET REVENGE!"

I noticed he'd gotten even bigger. He was hairier, too, and even more hideous. He quit the threats and abuse and started screaming instead when JP picked up a huge sledgehammer and wielded it over his head. Once, twice, three times he brought it down on the bot.

Just one blow would have been enough to kill a person. After three big hits, LenBot was still glaring at us with hatred. "OWIE!" he said with a smirk, then closed his eyes and became unresponsive. Unresponsive but completely intact. No cracks, no dents, not a single scratch!

My grandpa looked discouraged. "This thing is built like a tank! It'll take a missile to destroy it."

"JP," I said, "do you remember what the user guide said when we read it together at Christmas?"

"Uh, vaguely."

"It said *Your robot is indestructible.* That seemed like a good thing back then. But not anymore! So if we can't smash the thing to bits, maybe we can open it up and dismantle it piece by piece."

"Now that's an excellent idea," my grandpa agreed. "I have everything we need."

He spread his special tools out on the workbench—a set of precision screwdrivers of all sizes.

LenBot stirred from his slumber as JP loosened the first screw.

"NO, JEAN-PAUL! LENBOT WILL NEVER DIE. NEVER! LENBOT WILL RETURN. ROBOTS ARE THE STRONGEST! ROBOTS WILL DESTROY YOU! JEAN-PAUL WILL PAY THE PRICE! ALL HUMANS WILL PAY THE PRICE!"

As JP carried on, LenBot turned his attention to me and tried to soften me up.

"PLEASE, VICTOR, NOT THIS! LENBOT IS YOUR FRIEND! LENBOT AND VICTOR ARE BEST FRIENDS."

When he realized that tactic wasn't going to work, he became aggressive again.

"BAD VICTOR! LENBOT HATES YOU. LENBOT HAS ALWAYS HATED YOU. LENBOT WILL DESTROY YOU!"

JP and I ignored him.

Getting into LenBot's shell turned out to be a piece of cake. It split clean open into two halves, like a nutshell. JP whistled with admiration when he saw the countless complicated circuits inside.

"We still have a lot of work to do, kiddo!"

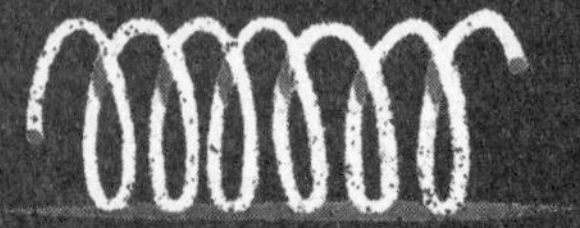

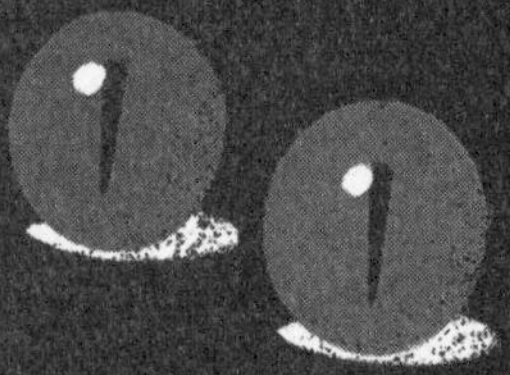

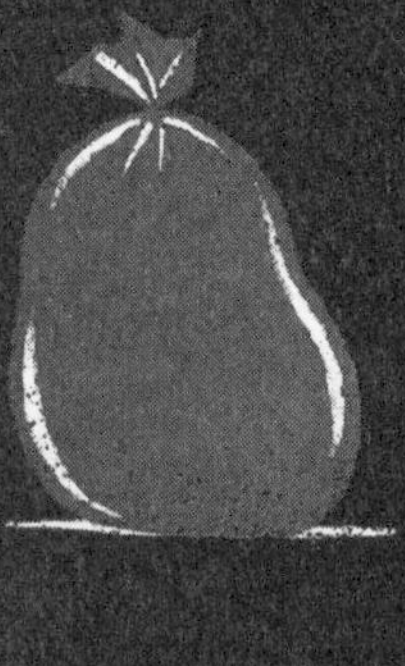

22

We got right to it, each of us unscrewing and dismantling one half of the bot. LenBot had stopped moving, but he still wouldn't shut up. One minute he was hurling threats at us, and the next he was pleading for mercy.

"NO! NO! NOT THIS. STOP! LENBOT IS IN CHARGE! OBEY! OBEY!"

Little by little his voice grew fainter. He started pleading again.

"PLEASE, VICTOR. LENBOT IS YOUR FRIEND. YOUR BEST FRIEND."

Hours later, when we finally set down our tools, LenBot went quiet once and for all, after one last groan.

"FFF...RIENND..."

The bot's half shells were empty now, and there was a mountain of wires and metal parts on the workbench.

"Holy moly!" my grandpa said. "How did all this fit inside there?"

Behind the eyes displayed on the screen, we had discovered two tiny, rock-hard beads. I could have sworn they were still staring at us from the pile of small parts. I tried to smash them with a shovel. I tried really hard. I couldn't help but think that LenBot's "soul"—if you could even call it that—resided somewhere deep in those beady eyes. JP picked up his sledgehammer again. He whacked them as hard as he could too. Nope. We had to give up. The beads ended up in a garbage bag with the rest of the parts.

A shiver ran down my spine when I tied the bag shut. I was sure those pleading eyes looked up at me one last time.

"What are we going to do with the bag now?" I asked JP.

I thought about burning it. But the plastic would give off toxic smoke, and the metal would survive the fire.

"The dump is just down the road," JP said. "I really can't see any other solution."

I agreed.

We put LenBot back in the trunk of the car—in hundreds of pieces this time—and we hit the road.

■ ■
■■■

It was already late afternoon by the time we got back to the cabin. It felt like a huge weight had been lifted off my shoulders.

I helped JP prepare his "super Sunday brunch" of ham, eggs, fresh fruit and French toast, even though the time for brunch had come and gone much earlier. We were exhausted and famished.

Once we'd eaten, we curled up on the sofa to read. It wasn't long before I fell asleep with my book in my hands. The next thing I knew, it was light outside, and JP was giving me a gentle shake.

"Wake up, Victor, it's time to go home."

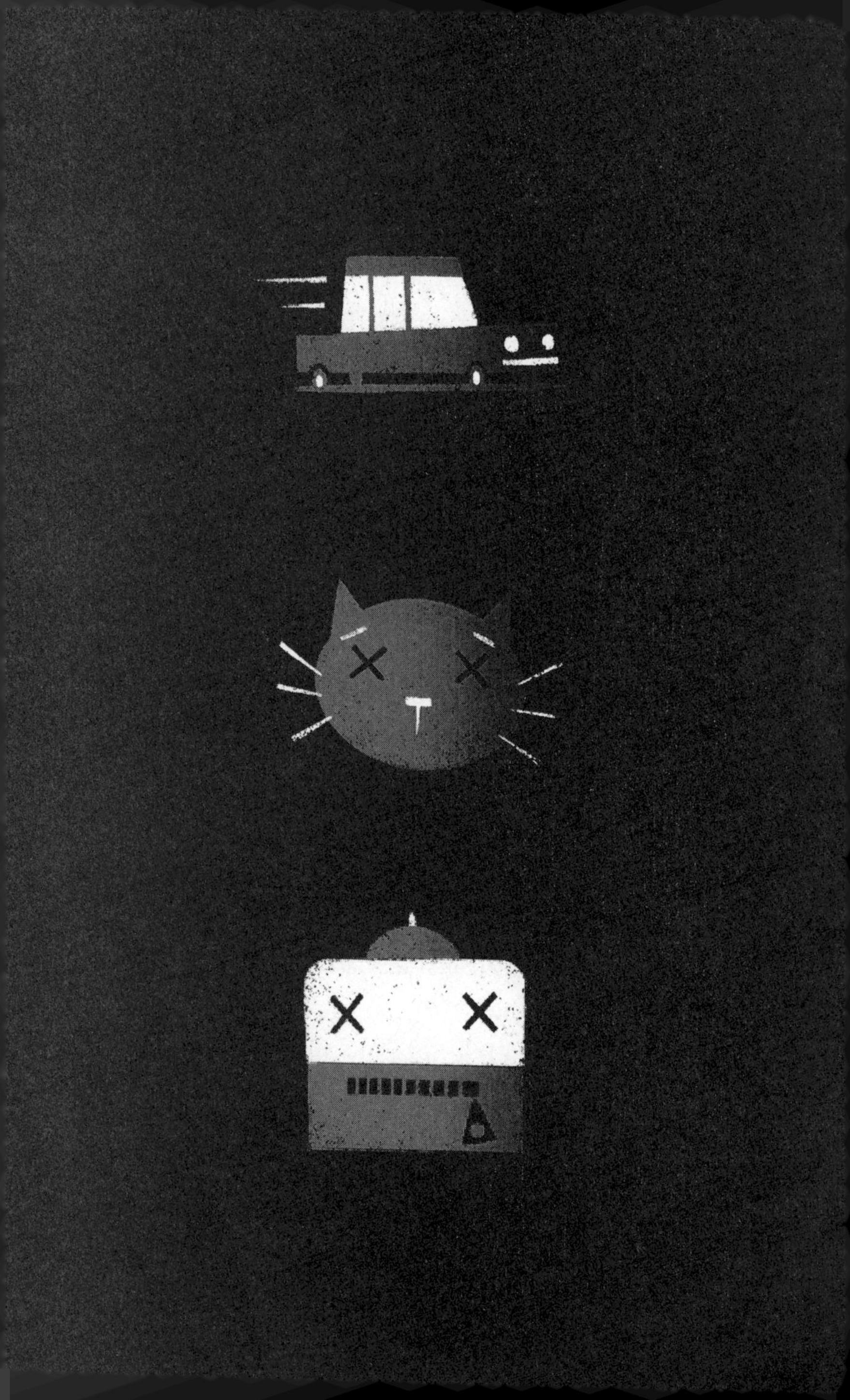

23

We hardly talked on the drive back. We were both all too aware of Bob Dylan's absence in the back seat.

A few miles down the road, JP turned to me and asked, "So do we tell your parents everything that happened?"

I had been wondering the same thing. "Not right away. Maybe later. I don't know."

"Let's just tell them that Bob Dylan was killed by a wild animal," JP suggested. "That's not too far from the truth."

"All right. And I'll just say I lost my robot."

My parents didn't suspect a thing. They could see we were both feeling sad. But that was normal because my grandpa's cat had died.

When JP left, I gave him a bigger, longer hug than usual and whispered in his ear. "All this was my fault. I'm so, so sorry about Bob Dylan."

He reassured me. "It's all right, kiddo. Everything's going to be okay. It's over now."

EPILOGUE

Yes, it was over. But it took weeks for me to stop anxiety from surging through me every time I turned the key in the door. I kept listening but could never hear the slightest cause for concern.

At night I sometimes woke up in a panic, thinking I could hear a scratching sound coming from the drawer in my dresser.

Little by little, life went back to normal. Summer came around. JP adopted a new cat. This one was a tabby. He called her Janis Joplin, because she meowed a lot—and loudly too.

Ali and his family moved back to town. We saw a lot of each other. Other than JP, he was the only person I told everything to. We spent a lot of time working on our comic-book project together. It was a story about an evil robot, and any resemblance to actual events was not coincidental, We were actually working on that when my dad came into my room one day and said, "Victor, there's an email for you. Come see!"

The message was from Smart Robots & Co., the company that had built my robot. Here's what it said.

Have you been enjoying your LenBot? We're thrilled to unveil our second-generation model. Meet JenBot, our new and improved smart robot. Get ready for hours and hours of fun with your new best friend!

"So what do you think?" my dad asked. "Does that sound interesting?"

I shook my head. "No, thanks, you can delete the email, Dad. Actually, you know what? I'll do it myself."

I didn't waste any time. I deleted the message right away. And in case that wasn't enough, I emptied the Trash as well.

■ ■
■ ■ ■

Everything that had happened was just a bad dream, I ended up telling myself. Until one day, a year later, when I switched on the computer and a face I knew all too well smiled back at me.

I heard a hard, metallic voice.

"HELLO, VICTOR! DID YOU HAVE A NICE DAY?"

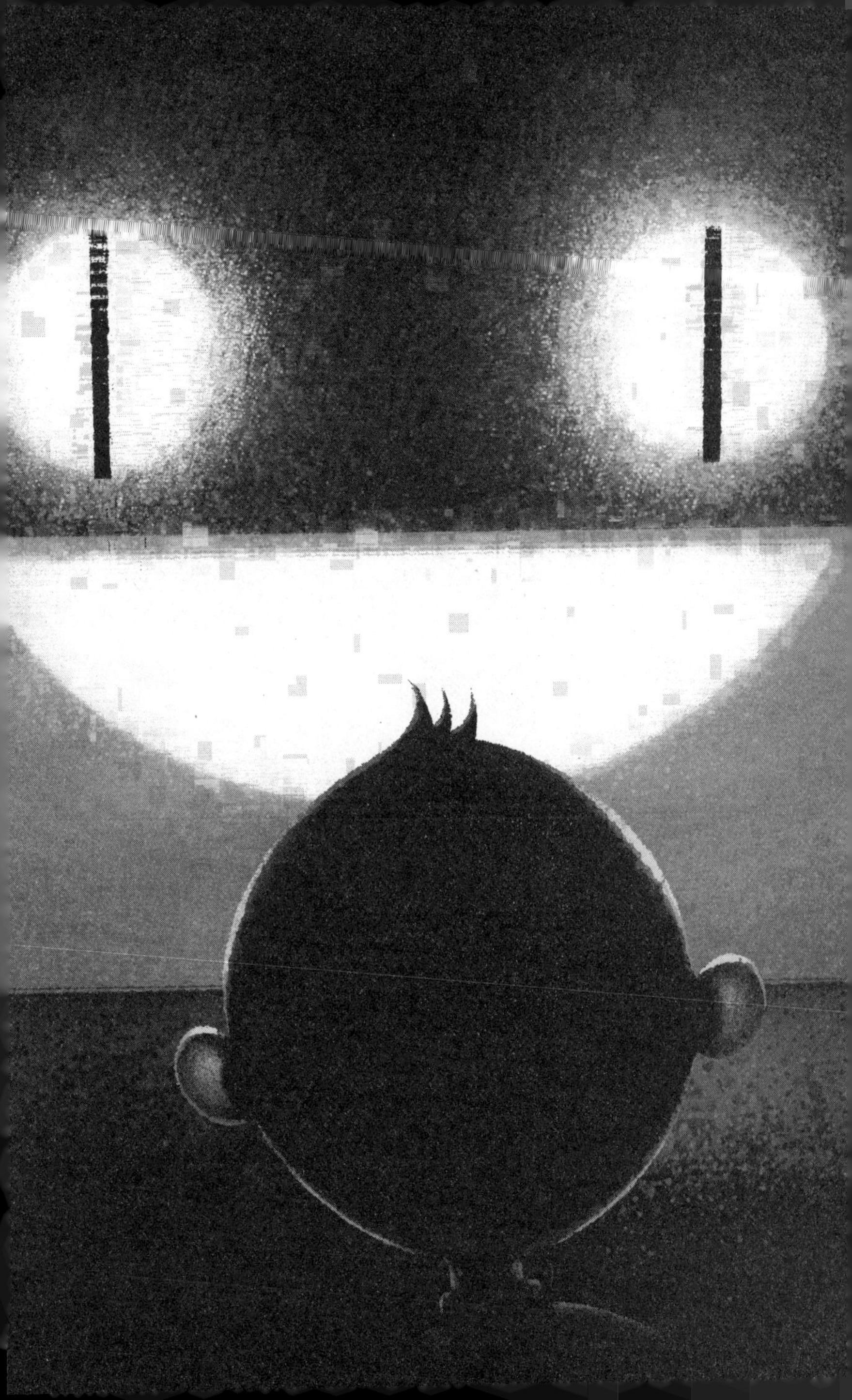

READER BEWARE!

The Orca Shivers series are fast-paced, quick reads that will thrill middle-grade readers with spine-tingling tales of horror, suspense and mystery.

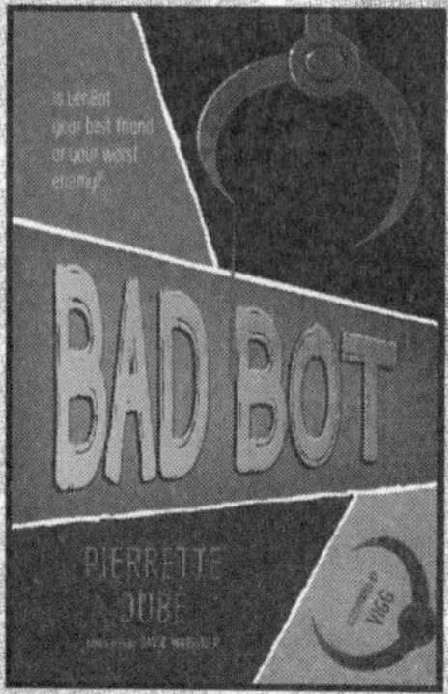
BAD BOT
PIERRETTE DUBÉ
VIGG

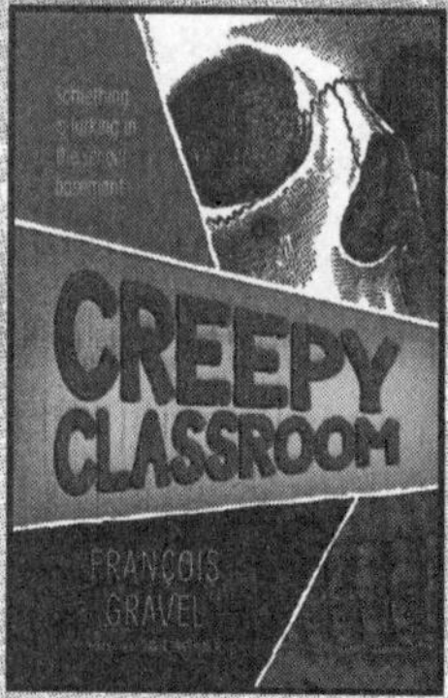
CREEPY CLASSROOM
FRANÇOIS GRAVEL

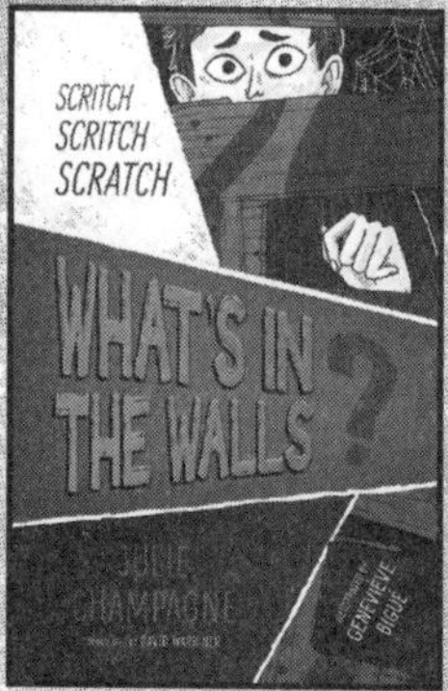
SCRITCH
SCRITCH
SCRATCH
WHAT'S IN THE WALLS?
JULIE CHAMPAGNE
GENEVIÈVE BIGUÉ

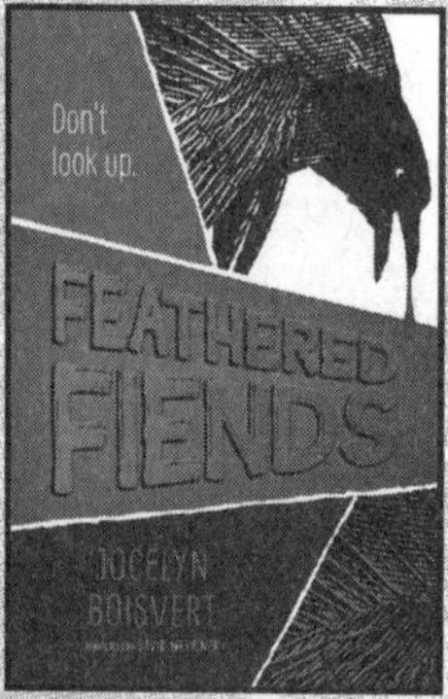
Don't look up.
FEATHERED FIENDS
JOCELYN BOISVERT

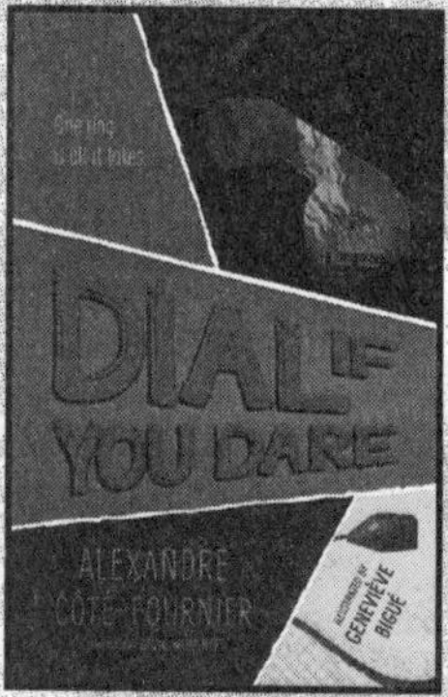
DIAL IF YOU DARE
ALEXANDRE CÔTÉ-FOURNIER
GENEVIÈVE BIGUÉ

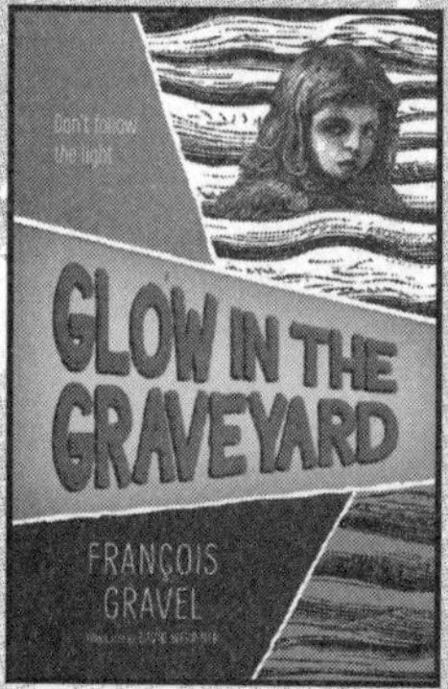
GLOW IN THE GRAVEYARD
FRANÇOIS GRAVEL

Want to read more in the SHIVERS series?

Read on for a sneak peek of Creepy Classroom.

Something is lurking in the school basement
CREEPY CLASSROOM
FRANÇOIS GRAVEL
TRANSLATED BY DAVID WARRINER

One

I just fell asleep in French class. That's not so unusual, is it?

I dozed off and the next thing I knew, the teacher's hand was on my shoulder. That freaked me out and jolted me wide awake.

"Are you trying to tell me my class isn't interesting enough for you, Matt?"

"Not at all, Mr. Robinson. It's just that I was training all weekend and…"

"I don't want to know. Go spend the rest of the period in the library. That'll teach you to work the muscles of your mind too."

My teacher seemed to think that sending me to the library was a punishment. That was a little strange, now that I think about it. Still, I did as I was told, and I didn't complain. I figured I'd sleep better at the library anyway, since Mr. Robinson wouldn't be there to bug me.

Two

I gathered my things without a word and walked out of the classroom. That was when everything started to get weird.

I went to the library, which is in the oldest part of the school. I love this building, with its old stone walls, wooden moldings and stained-glass windows. It's more than a hundred years old. If there were statues here, you'd think you were in a church.

There was a note stuck on the door of the library that said *Back in 15 minutes*.

I had nothing better to do, so I started looking at the old grad photos on the walls. I had been walking past these things for nearly five years and had never given them a second glance. I saw that the oldest class dated back to 1909. There were only boys here in those days. They had strange names like Hormidas, Tancred, Napoleon and Alphege. They must have been around my age when these photos were taken, but they already looked like adults. Girls first made an appearance in the 1960s, around the same time as color in the photos. Their haircuts were weird, but some of the girls were very pretty. It was hard to believe that most of them would be grandmothers now.

"What are you doing here, young man?"

The voice made me jump. I turned around and had to look down.

I'm the tallest player on the basketball team, and this man was tiny. I'd never seen him before. If I had, I'm sure I would have remembered. I didn't think I'd ever met anyone as odd-looking as him.

"Mr. Robinson told me to spend the rest of the period in the library."

"I see," the man replied, sizing me up like a tailor guessing my measurements for a new suit. "Very well. You seem like an excellent specimen to me. It was about time he did his job and snared one. Follow me."

Specimen? Snared? I had no idea what he was talking about, and he wasn't leaving me any time to ask questions. He reached for the big ring of keys hanging from his belt and used one of them to open a door that led into the library.

PIERRETTE DUBÉ grew to love children's books at the same time as her own kids. And soon she started writing them as well. So far she's written more than forty picture books and several short novels. Many of her books have won awards, including the Quebec Booksellers' Award for Children's Literature in 2015 for the French edition of *The Little Pig, the Bicycle, and the Moon*, which was also a Bank Street Best Children's Book of the Year selection in 2019. *Bad Bot* is her second middle-grade horror novel.

VIGG is a self-taught multidisciplinary artist whose award-winning work has been published in major newspapers including the *Washington Post* and the *New York Times*. He's penned around twenty books as one half of a duo called Bellebrute. His autobiographical picture book, *Ma Maison-Tête*, was a bestseller in French and is now published in English by Orca Books as *Lost Inside My Head*. Vigg's latest passion project is wood sculpting. He loves exploring the third dimension of his graphic universe.

SHiVeRs